A Horse Called

Tamarindo

BOOKS BY JOANNE CHITWOOD NOWACK:

A Horse Called Mayonnaise
A Horse Called Blackberry
A Horse Called Poppyseed
A Horse Called Tamarindo

To order, call 1-800-765-6955.

Visit our website at *www.rhpa.org* for information on other Review and Herald products.

A Horse Called Tamarindo

JoAnne Chitwood Nowack

Sequel to *A Horse Called Poppyseed*

REVIEW AND HERALD® PUBLISHING ASSOCIATION
HAGERSTOWN, MD 21740

The author assumes full responsibility for the accuracy
of all facts and quotations as cited in this book.

This book was
Edited by Penny Estes Wheeler
Designed by Willie Duke
Cover illustration by Scott Snow
Electronic makeup by Shirley M. Bolivar
Typeset: 12.5/14 Times New Roman

PRINTED IN U.S.A.

04 03 02 01 00   5 4 3 2 1

R&H Cataloging Service
Nowack, JoAnne Chitwood
    A horse called Tamarindo.

    I. Title.

                813.54

ISBN 0-8280-1499-X

DEDICATION

To Jason, Heidi, and Emily
who have the gift
of making each day
a true adventure.

CHAPTER ONE

The old pickup truck lurched to a stop. Tory rubbed away a small patch of the fog that had collected on her passenger window and peered out at the rainy landscape. Scrawny hens, drenched from the steady downpour, scratched in the red mud. A dismal cement-block building squatted beside the road, as if some giant child had placed it there, then carelessly forgot to put it away.

"Not much to look at, is it?"

Tory turned to the tall, sandy-haired man driving the pickup and shook her head. "No, Mr. Allen, it surely isn't." A mosquito landed on her arm looking for a free lunch. She swatted at it but missed. "Are we in Mexico yet?"

Bart Allen chuckled. "Don't I wish. This is the inspection station for the border crossing. We're still in Texas. I just hope it doesn't take too long." He gave Tory a long look. "Is this your first time out of the country?"

Tory shook her head and smiled. "No. I've been to Canada several times. But that probably doesn't count, because it's so much like the United States." She glanced out the window at the barren landscape just in time to see a pack of skinny dogs dart across the road and into a scraggly patch of underbrush. "I've never been anywhere like this, though. Is this what Honduras is like?"

"I don't know," Mr. Allen said quietly as he reached for his door handle. "Linda and I have never been there before, either." He winked at Tory as he stepped out into the rain. "Don't worry, though. We'll make a great team at the orphanage with your nursing skills, Linda's cooking expertise, and my knowledge of construction. And then there's Adam." He flashed her a smile as he scurried toward the block building, his coat pulled up over his head to protect him from the driving rain.

Adam. Tory turned the name over and over in her mind like a rubix cube puzzle searching for clues about the young man she'd be working with for the next year. Anna Giles, from Outreach International, had told her that he'd be working with her and the Allens, but had given no further details. She thought of her friend Robyn's last words to her as Tory had said goodbye to her and to her mare and colt, Peaches and Poppyseed. "You're going to be working so closely with this guy, Adam, that you'll either end up best friends or hate each other." She smiled at the memory. *I just hope Adam and I get along OK. Never mind being best friends.*

The driver's door of the pickup opened suddenly, and Linda Allen slid onto the seat, giggling as she shook the rain from her short, golden-brown hair. Although Tory had only known the woman a few hours, she liked her already. Her cheerful smile and upbeat attitude gave her the appearance of someone much younger than her 30-something years.

"I have supper almost ready in the camper," Linda said as she glanced toward the door of the block building where her husband had disappeared. "I hope he comes out soon. Are you hungry?"

"Starved!" Tory's stomach rumbled. She patted it and laughed. "I've been so caught up in all the new sights and sounds I almost forgot I haven't eaten since Mom and Dad dropped me off this morning."

"Well, we'll have to remedy that." Linda opened the door and hopped out into the rain. "Come on. We'll eat now and save a plate for Bart."

Tory followed Linda through the mud to the camper door in the back of the pickup. She tried not to think about the mess the thick, red muck was making of her new Adidas. As she pulled herself up onto the camper step, she slid the slimy shoes from her feet and tucked them in an out of the way corner of the entryway.

The rich odor of spaghetti sauce and garlic bread filled the camper as Linda placed a steaming bowl of freshly cooked spaghetti on the tiny camp table. She reached into a drawer beside the propane stove and pulled out a handful of plastic silverware and a tuft of paper napkins and plopped them on top of a stack of paper plates.

"Here you go. Make yourself useful," she said, handing the pile to Tory.

Tory arranged three plates and three sets of utensils around the table. "Here are the extras." She held out the spare knife, fork, spoon, and plate.

Linda smiled and shook her head. "No, they aren't extra. Go ahead and set four places. Adam should be here any minute and from what I know of him, the first item of importance on his list of things to do will be *eating.*"

Just then the camper door swung open and Mr. Allen's face appeared in the doorway. "Hey, is that food I smell? We've got two hungry men here. Adam is back with the little truck, loaded with supplies. Isn't that right, Adam?"

A tall, slender young man with short, dark hair and serious blue eyes joined Bart in the doorway. "That's right. It's all loaded," he said. His voice was heavy with fatigue. "That was a long drive. I wasn't sure part of the time if I was going to make it. Good thing my angel works overtime."

Both men removed their shoes and squeezed in around the little table. As Adam sat down, he looked straight at Tory, a quizzical expression on his face.

"Oh, I'm sorry." Mr. Allen put an arm around Adam's shoulder. "I forgot you two haven't met. Tory, this is Adam Hartman. Adam, this is Tory Butler."

"Hi, Adam." Tory smiled and reached out a hand for him to shake.

Adam extended his hand, too. His hand was big and felt warm and strong as Tory gripped it, but she saw no hint of warmth or welcome in his eyes. They looked distant and preoccupied.

Oh no, we're not going to be friends. Tory shifted her focus to her spaghetti and didn't say another word the rest of the meal. When she got up to clear the dishes after everyone finished eating, she noticed that Adam's plate was almost untouched.

Darkness fell quickly as Tory helped Linda and Adam repack and rearrange boxes and bags of clothing and supplies for the orphanage while Mr. Allen negotiated the border crossing with the guards. Between the camper, the trailer that the Allens were pulling behind the pickup, and the little silver Toyota pickup, it seemed that there would be plenty of room for all the baggage. But when they were finished, every nook and cranny was stuffed with something with not a square inch of space to spare. Through all the work of packing and repacking, Tory and Adam worked side by side, but Adam never said a word to her.

It was almost midnight when Tory, exhausted, finally crawled into her sleeping bag in the front of the pickup. The light from the Coleman lantern they had used for their packing work still flickered from the cab of the Toyota. She sat up for a few moments with the warm down bag scrunched up around her neck and watched the light reflect on the rain droplets as they forged crooked little paths down the truck windshield. She saw Adam toss his sleeping bag onto the seat of the Toyota, climb in, and quietly close the door. Tory suspected that the Allens were already asleep in their makeshift bed in the camper, but she liked Adam's thoughtfulness in trying not to disturb them. She snuggled down into her sleeping bag, curling up in the only position she could find that kept the gearshift stick from jabbing into her side.

Good night, Father, she prayed. *Thanks for an interesting day. I'd like to ask one little favor, though. Could Adam and I please somehow be friends?*

The next thing she knew, Tory opened her eyes to bright sunlight streaming into the cab of the pickup. She sat up just in time to see Mr. Allen striding toward the truck, a worried frown on his face. Slipping out of her sleeping bag, she pulled her shoes on and swung the pickup door open.

"What's happening?" she asked.

He shook his head. "Oh, it's just all this red tape we have to go through to get across the border. Now they're telling me that we have to get all of our belongings inventoried and have an official seal placed on the trailer. We may not be able to leave until tomorrow morning."

Just then Linda came around the corner of the camper, a Texas map in her hand. "I have an idea, Bart," she said, excited. "Padre Island is just a few miles away and here's a campground right on the water. Tomorrow's Friday and by the time we finish up here, it will be almost Sabbath. Let's just spend the Sabbath in a beautiful, peaceful place and cross the border when it opens again on Monday."

Mr. Allen nodded. "I'd be OK with that. It could be our reward for all this work packing and repacking everything. What do you think, Tory?"

"Sure!" Tory imagined herself dangling her toes in the turquoise water of the Gulf of Mexico. The prospect of spending a whole day relaxing on the beach sounded almost too good to be true.

The rest of that day sped by. It seemed that every town official had to approve their cargo and the requirements for the border crossing seemed to change with each person who inspected the trailer. One young Mexican man who completed a detailed inventory of the contents of the trucks and the trailer knew some English and talked with Tory as he worked. He introduced himself as Mario.

"Where are you going?" Mario asked as he opened a box of pots and pans, carefully placing each one on the concrete slab that was his only work space. Tory explained the work of the orphanage in Santa Barbara and how she had felt a distinct call from God to go there.

"This God you speak of," Mario said thoughtfully, "you talk about Him as if you know Him. How can you know Someone you can't see?"

Tory sent up a quick prayer for wisdom. *Let them be Your words, Father. Reach out to Mario through me, please.* As she prayed, an image of a letter flashed into her mind. "Have you ever had a pen pal?" she asked.

Mario flashed a smile, his white teeth bright against his handsome dark face. "Si. I know this word *pen pal*. When I go to school, we write letters to children in other places. I write to a boy in Alaska."

"Did you become friends with the boy?" Tory pulled another box from the trailer.

"Si. I know all about his family and his life."

Tory smiled. "You talk about him as if you know him. How can you know someone you can't see?"

Mario stopped in his tracks. "So you are saying you get letters from this God you talk of?"

"Just a moment, Mario," Tory said. She hurried to the front of the pickup and reached in through the open window. She knew Mr. Allen kept a supply of Spanish New Testaments and little booklets called *Steps to Christ,* also translated into Spanish, in the glove compartment. She pulled out one of each.

"This is God's letter to me," Tory said, holding the New Testament out to Mario. "And this is another book that tells about how to be friends with Jesus, God's Son." She handed him the other book. "God wants to be friends with you, too."

Tory could see tears in Mario's eyes as he accepted the books. He brushed them away quickly, and she sensed that he'd been waiting for someone to talk to about God. He continued his work in contemplative silence and Tory kept quiet too, not wishing to break into his thoughts with her words.

Father, she prayed, *is Mario one of the people You sent me to talk to? Please work in his life and help him to find someone in his own town that he can talk to about You.*

Tory climbed into the trailer to pull out one of the last boxes and almost bumped into Adam. He grinned. "Hey, Tory. Good job unloading the trailer. I've almost got everything emptied out of both trucks, too." He looked straight at her for the first time since they met the first night.

"Thanks," she said. "It feels good to be getting to the end of it. I was beginning to think we'd be stuck here forever and never see Honduras."

Adam laughed. "Yeah. It's a pain to get through the border sometimes, especially if you're taking lots of stuff." He waved his arm toward the piles of bags and boxes on the concrete slab. "I lived in Honduras when I was little and we go back pretty frequently, so I've been through this before. This too shall pass."

"So you know Spanish?"

"Yep. I mean *Si,* senorita," Adam chuckled at Tory's expression. "Don't you know any Spanish?"

Tory shook her head. "I learned a little in grade school, but I don't remember much. I've been hoping to find someone who could give me a crash course before I have to depend on my language skills for survival."

"Well, allow me to introduce myself as your new Spanish tutor," Adam said, sticking out his hand for Tory to shake. "That is, if you want me to be. I was kind of grumpy the first day we were together. Those horrid malaria pills make me so sick." He dropped his gaze and began to dig a little hole in the red mud with the toe of his boot.

It's not that he doesn't like me, Tory suddenly realized. *He's actually afraid I won't like him.*

Tory grasped Adam's hand and smiled. "I would be honored to be your student, *Senor.*"

CHAPTER TWO

Sabbath morning dawned clear and sunny over South Padre Island. Tory sat in the cab of the pickup, her journal in her lap. She chewed on the end of her pencil as she tried to think of what to say about the trip so far. *It's so beautiful here on Padre Island,* she wrote, *as perfect and peaceful as that border town felt ugly and desolate. It seems as if nothing bad could ever happen here.*

Seagulls screamed insults to each other as they wheeled through the sky above the docks. Majestic sailboats, their polished wooden bows gleaming golden in the morning sun, rocked gently in their moorings. The turquoise water shimmered against the white sand. Tory sighed and wrote, *This is surely an island paradise. I wonder if anywhere in Honduras is this spectacular.*

She heard a tap on the window beside her and turned to see Adam's face pressed against the glass. She rolled down the window. "Hey, you're leaving nose prints on my bedroom window glass," she teased.

"Oops, sorry," Adam said, in mock repentance. "It's time to seize the day. Why don't you come walking with me?"

"OK," Tory agreed as she rolled the window back up and got out of the truck.

"Do you want to go exploring?"

"Sure."

They walked quickly to the beach, then along the white sand. Within minutes the curve of the shoreline took them completely out of view of the camp site. It seemed they'd followed the shore for at least an hour when Tory spotted a sign nailed to a weatherbeaten post. "Hey, this says we're in the Padre Island wildlife reserve."

Adam pointed to a stubby tree with scaly grey bark growing at the water's edge. "Let's climb it." Without waiting for her to answer, he sprinted to the tree and shimmied up the trunk. He perched on a thick branch, pretending to be a pirate searching the horizon for enemy ships. "Yo, ho, ho and a bottle of cran-raspberry juice," he chanted, grasping the branch with one hand and shading his eyes with the other. "Methinks there is nothing in this wildlife reserve but birds."

Tory laughed. "What did you expect, giraffes?" She reached the tree just as he climbed to a higher branch. "Coming up!" she called.

The rough bark cut into her hands as she pulled herself up to one of the lower branches. She looked out over the water, amazed at how much further she could see. A skiff, its miniature sail trimmed in the stiff breeze, glided by like a toy set in motion by some giant unseen hand. Tory watched it pass, then reached for the next branch.

Adam reached over and patted the branch opposite his. "Come on up, tree climber. Have a seat here."

When she'd situated herself comfortably on the branch, Tory turned to Adam. "What made you decide to go back to Honduras?" She hoped he didn't mind answering such a personal question. She thought of how worried she'd been when Adam first arrived, that he wouldn't want to be her friend. Now here she was sitting in a tree with him, talking as if they'd known each other forever.

Adam stared out across the water for a few moments,

and Tory began to wonder if he'd even heard her question. Finally he turned to her. "I don't know how to explain it," he said thoughtfully. "Call it a strong impression or an unquenchable urge. I just knew I was supposed to go. This year. Now."

Tory nodded. "I can relate to that. It was that way for me, too."

"It's a sure sign of adventure ahead," Adam said, his blue eyes sparkling. Suddenly he stood up on his branch with his tanned arms outstretched, balancing himself precariously. He dropped to all fours, grasped the branch, and swung into a back flip to the ground below.

"Whew!" Tory let out an appreciative whistle. "Where did you learn to do that?" She climbed gingerly down from the tree, taking one branch at a time.

Adam grinned. "Acrosports in college. I'll teach you if you want to learn."

"Sure. I *do* like adventure." Tory pulled several pieces of bark from her palms. "I think."

Early on Monday morning, Mr. Allen drove the Ford pickup into line at the Mexican border crossing. Tory rode with the Allens, and Adam drove the Toyota. Tory stared in amazement at the 20-foot fence, topped with razor sharp pieces of metal and rolled barbed wire, that guarded the American side of the border.

After what seemed like hours of inching forward, Mr. Allen finally pulled under a large canopy beside the border guards' office and produced visas and papers for the vehicles. The guards inspected the trailer and each of the vehicles and waved them forward. They crossed a wide, shallow river, its brown water meandering through the valley. It reminded Tory of chocolate milk. Which reminded her that she was thirsty with no immediate prospects of finding something to drink.

On the other side of the river lay "no man's land," a long, barren strip of ground that neither country claimed. "It helps the soldiers maintain the border," Mr. Allen explained. Just beyond "no man's land" they reached the Mexican border patrol office. Several soldiers in green uniforms, carrying M-16's as casually as if they were water pistols, stood around the office compound. The soldiers watched intently as two Mexican border guards inspected the papers Mr. Allen held out. The papers must have been satisfactory, because the guards waved the group on without further delay.

Tory watched the passing landscape as they drove into Mexico. They crossed another river with palm trees lining its banks. Women beat their clothing clean with rocks at the river's edge. Tory thought of how she complained about doing laundry at home with a washer and dryer. Pulling her journal out of the book bag at her feet, she wrote, *Something tells me I'm about to experience an attitude adjustment about the "necessities" of life. I wonder if the women in Honduras do their laundry this way?*

The sun climbed higher in the sky and the landscape grew more and more parched. Stately saguaro cactuses lifted spiny arms to the cloudless sky as if placing requests for rain. Just when the pickup gas tank registered empty and Tory was beginning to think they were going to have to walk to find gas, a cluster of tiny houses appeared. A Shell sign from the 1950's balanced precariously on a fence post next to an old gas pump.

The gas station attendant was a friendly sort, pushing his weather-beaten straw hat back on his head and flashing them a toothless grin. Several young children played in the dirt nearby. He spoke to them and they scattered, disappearing into the dilapidated building behind the gas pump. He gestured toward the building and rattled off something in Spanish.

"What's he saying?" Tory asked Adam, who had climbed from the Toyota and was stretching his back and legs.

"He's letting us know there's cold soda pop in the gas station." Adam glanced longingly back toward the building. "Sounds good, huh?"

But before they could take a step, the children ran toward them, each carrying a glass bottle. One little boy held a bottle out to Tory, and a tiny girl with a red ribbon in her long black hair held one out to Adam. The man spoke a few more words that Tory couldn't understand, and the children turned back to the building again, this time carrying bottles of cold soda pop to Linda and Mr. Allen. Mr. Allen reached in his pocket for some coins to pay him. The man shook his head and began talking very rapidly.

"He's giving the drinks to us as a gift," Adam said, surprise registering on his face. "These people are dirt poor and he wants to give *us* a gift."

"Gracias." Tory smiled at the man. *"Muchas gracias."*

Mr. Allen and Linda nodded and smiled, too. *"Sí. Muchas gracias."*

Tory turned to the cab of the pickup and reached into her book bag. She found a braided bookmark she'd made from silky blue and green cord and tiny silver glass beads. Then she grabbed one of her pens, a green and white one with a rubber Garfield head on the end. She held the bookmark out to the little girl and the pen to the boy. They stepped forward and shyly accepted the gifts. The man beamed and nodded his appreciation. *"Gracias, gracias,"* he repeated over and over.

As the afternoon wore on, the little caravan traveled farther and farther into Mexico's interior. Tory noticed that the road became more and more rutted, sometimes deteriorating to little more than a cow path. Mr. Allen drove slowly, avoiding huge potholes that loomed up every few hundred feet. Then without warning a huge brown and white spotted pig with at least a dozen pink squealing piglets charged from the mesquite scrub and across the road in front of the truck. Mr. Allen slammed on his brakes.

"Something tells me we're approaching a village," he said, laughing nervously. "It's a good thing there aren't any elephants in Mexico."

Linda patted his arm. "Hey, good job saving the bacon," she teased.

Tory laughed along with her. By this time, two chickens and a tawny colored pigmy goat had joined the cow. Mr. Allen just leaned over the steering wheel looking back and forth from the menagerie in the road to his laughing wife. "I don't know why they have to collect in the *road,*" he said, shaking his head in bewilderment.

He maneuvered the pickup around the animal road block, motioning back to Adam to follow. He turned down a narrow road that crossed a dry creek bed and wound its way down to a grove of some kind of willow that grew along the creek at the valley floor. Just beyond the valley, a high plateau rose like a sentinel above the sparse landscape.

Tory gasped at the beauty of the scene. Until now, the countryside had been mostly dry and barren, dotted with cactus and patches of scrub mesquite. Here, the hillside stretched up vivid green. A waterfall cascaded down the rocky slope and into a pool bordered by lush flowering plants. An old hotel nestled at the base of the hill.

Mr. Allen glanced at Linda and Tory and raised his eyebrows. "So who will have the last laugh today? How's this for a place to camp tonight?"

CHAPTER THREE

"Ah. Now this is more like it." Tory sighed blissfully as she sank up to her neck in the cool water. Luxuriant tropical plants lined the walkway around the pool, their thick greenery illuminated by tiki torches placed every few feet along the stone path. A cascade of water plunged into the pool on the south end, creating an explosion of tiny bubbles.

Adam swam slowly toward her in the dark water with just the top of his head and his eyes showing above the surface. Tory swam backward away from him, giggling. "Adam, what are you doing?" She turned and pulled hard toward the waterfall. Glancing back, she saw him gaining on her. Suddenly, he rose out of the water with a roar, held his hands up in front of his face as if they were snapping jaws and clamped them on her arm.

"Alligator!" he shouted, dissolving into laughter. "Haven't you ever played alligator?" he asked.

Tory shook her head, still shocked. "No, I don't think so."

"I used to play it all the time with my brother," Adam said, holding his sides from laughing.

Tory noticed the look of nostalgia that flitted over Adam's face. "Do you miss him?" she asked softly.

"Yeah, I do." Adam swam to the edge of the pool, pulled himself out, and grabbed his towel. "A lot, actually. Although I never thought I'd hear myself admit it.

He's in the Army now, in Korea. I pray for him every day and just hope he's OK. What about you? Do you have anybody you miss like that?"

Tory shrugged as she swam in place, using her hands as flippers to keep her above water. "My folks, I guess. And my kids." She smiled at Adam's look of surprise and quickly added, "My horses, I mean. I also have an adopted calf that thinks I'm his mom." Paddling to the edge of the pool, she climbed out. The cool evening breeze on her wet skin made her shiver.

Adam handed her a towel and she wrapped it around her shoulders. "Tell me about your horses," he said. He sat down on the stone path next to the pool. Tory sat beside him, pulling the towel close around her for warmth.

"Their names are Peaches and Poppyseed," she explained. "I had to leave them with my friend, Robyn." She went on to describe the mare and colt and how she'd trained Poppyseed from the time he was a newborn foal. Then she told him about Cool Springs Camp, Mayonnaise and Blackberry, and her adventures with Brian and Mike on the pack trips.

"Wow," Adam said, a deeper tone of respect in his voice. "You *do* like adventure, don't you? Well, I hope you get to ride as much as you want to in Honduras. I've heard the orphanage has a horse."

Tory's heart jumped. "You're kidding!" she gasped. "I didn't expect to even *see* a horse in Honduras, much less get to ride."

"Oh, yes," Adam said, smiling at Tory's excitement, "there are horses in Honduras. But don't expect them to look like the horses you're used to in the States. Most people have a hard enough time keeping beans and rice on the table. They don't have extra money for anything for the horses to eat. They pretty much fend for themselves. They aren't usually even fenced in." He sighed and his eyes filled with pain for a moment. "I've seen them hit by cars or buses in the road. It's sad."

Tory shuddered. "That's terrible." She pictured Peaches and Poppyseed wandering up and down dirt roads scavenging for food in the sparse countryside. How could such a beautiful place hold such cruelty?

The eastern sky barely shimmered a rosy gold over the violet hills the next morning when Mr. Allen rolled everyone out of their sleeping bags to begin the day's journey. Tory groaned when her feet hit the hard cold ground. After her relaxing swim the night before, she felt as if she could sleep until noon. She was thankful for the five-gallon jugs of water that Mr. Allen was able to buy in the little town. By noon the temperature would soar into the 90s.

After a quick breakfast of fresh pineapple and coarse-grained Mexican pastries, the little entourage was on its way. The scenery in this part of Mexico was vastly different from what they'd driven through so far. It was as if they had crossed some invisible line between desert and jungle. Everywhere Tory looked she saw vivid green foliage and brightly colored flowering plants. Small stands made of twigs and sticks dotted the roadside, bananas and plantains hanging by their stalks in the windowless openings.

Mr. Allen pulled off the road next to one of the fruit stands and motioned Adam over. "Let's get some fresh fruit," he said eagerly. "It should be safe to eat bananas and oranges here because they have a removable peeling."

Tory wandered into the little stand. A wrinkled old woman sat in the corner behind a rickety table. Two chickens pecked at an orange peel on the ground by her feet, and a tiny baby, its thick hair as dark as the black threads in the hammock that held it suspended, slept peacefully, unaware of her presence. Tory pulled a bunch of tiny bananas from their stalk and held them up to the woman. *"¿Quanto questa?"* she asked. "How much?"

The woman held up two fingers, but Tory wasn't sure if she meant pesos or one of the smaller Mexican coins. She fished in her pocket for some Mexican coins and placed several of them in the woman's hand. The woman took the two smallest coins and gave the others back.

Just as Tory peeled back the tough skin of one of the tiny bananas, Adam peered in through one of the openings in the wall of the enclosure. "There you are," he said to Tory. Then, seeing the banana in her hand, a slow smile spread over his face. "Go ahead, eat it," he said, still grinning. "It's an unforgettable experience, trust me."

Tory looked down at the banana, then back at Adam. "You just want me to give it to you," she said, wrinkling up her nose at him. "Well, you're out of luck. *I'm* eating this one." With that she popped the little morsel of fruit into her mouth.

As soon as the banana hit her tongue, Tory felt her mouth start to pucker and a horrible, bitter, chalky taste filled her mouth. She gagged and ran outside, coughing and choking, spitting the horrible tasting fruit onto the ground. Adam's laughter sounded as if it came from somewhere far away. Her head spun and nausea gripped her.

It took several minutes for the nausea to pass and the hideous chalkiness to subside in her mouth. Adam stepped out from the fruit stand peeling a large orange. He held a section out to Tory. "Here. This will help get the taste out of your mouth."

Tory accepted the orange slice and carefully put it into her mouth. It did seem to help. Then she stared straight at Adam. *"You knew,"* she said icily. "You knew it was horrible and that I would be so-o-o sorry I ate it."

Adam laughed. "Yes, I knew." He handed her another slice of orange." Ask me *how* I knew. Everyone has to have it happen to them at least once or their tropical experience just isn't complete."

"I guess I forgive you." Tory sucked on the orange slice and shuddered. "I wouldn't want to go through life with an *incomplete* tropical experience, now would I?"

"Welcome to Mexico," Mr. Allen said, laughing. Tory scowled. "Sorry," he said, still chuckling as he got in the truck and started the engine.

They drove for miles up a winding narrow road with tall rock bluffs on either side. It wasn't until they reached the top that Tory realized they'd been climbing up onto a huge plateau. Once they reached the top, the view took her breath away. Layer after layer of gently rolling mountains stretched for miles in every direction.

They drove through the mountains the rest of the day, and on into the next. After going up and down a particularly long hill, suddenly the truck engine coughed and sputtered. Mr. Allen pulled over, and Tory saw Adam pulling the Toyota over behind them. The two men lifted the hood of the pickup to check out the engine. When they finally slammed it shut, Mr. Allen shook his head. Tory thought she heard him murmur to Adam "pray that we make it."

The next few miles of road were flat, and the truck seemed to have decided to behave and cause no more problems. Reaching the opposite end of the plateau, Tory saw a huge green valley stretching out before them. The truck picked up speed on the steep descent, and Mr. Allen pumped the brakes to keep the truck from going too fast on the curves. At one point, a strange burning smell wafted into the cab. Then it went away, and Tory didn't think anything more about it.

When they crossed the Guatemalan border, Tory felt as if they'd entered a different world. The same high fences guarded "no man's land," but the people looked entirely different. Aztec Indians in their brightly colored native dress filled the streets, and children hit the truck as they drove by, calling out in their native language. A huge stone wall with a tangle of hanging vines stood at the edge of the jungle, like a gate to a strange new land. Stone statues lined the road and tropical birds and monkeys filled the trees above.

Huge potholes loomed every few hundred yards in the steep, winding road. Mr. Allen gripped the steering wheel until his knuckles were white, as huge buses and trucks whooshed past with no apparent respect for the condition of the road. The road grew steeper as they headed down into a canyon. Dark gray rock walls towered on one side of the road, and a ragged cliff fell off to the river below on the other. The burning smell grew stronger, and suddenly Mr. Allen gasped in a voice tight with fear, "Our brakes are going out."

Tory held her breath and prayed as she watched the vines on the side of the road speed by faster and faster. Mr. Allen pumped the brakes, and all at once they caught and the truck slowed. He pulled over into a small clearing beside the road just as an eighteen-wheeler that had been riding his bumper thundered past.

Adam's ashen face appeared in Tory's window, and she rolled it down. "What's going on?" he asked, his voice shaking. "Why were you going so fast?"

"The brakes went out," Mr. Allen explained. He let

out a deep breath. "Wow. What a place for it to happen, too. Maybe we won't get blown off the road until they have a chance to cool down."

Mr. Allen, Linda, and Tory got out of the truck and joined Adam on the roadside. They stood as far away from the lanes of traffic as they could. Behind them, dense foliage lined the crevice between cliffs. *It's beautiful, but it's spooky,* Tory thought as she peered into the dark jungle. A brightly colored parrot flew over her head.

A car pulled off the road just behind the Toyota, and a well-dressed man got out and motioned to Mr. Allen and Adam. Tory could tell by watching the men's faces that the topic of conversation was very serious. The strange man talked, then Adam interpreted for Mr. Allen. In just a few moments the man quickly jumped back into his car and left.

Mr. Allen and Adam hurried over to Tory and Linda. "It's bandits," Mr. Allen said quietly. "That man says this is a favorite spot for bandits to raid unsuspecting motorists who have car trouble. They hide in that jungle right there."

Tory felt her stomach flip over with fear. *Bandits.* She had read stories in the newspaper about the kinds of things bandits in Central America did to their victims. Would they even make it to Honduras? Would she ever see her family again?

"I think it's time to pray," Mr. Allen said, his voice suddenly confident and firm. The four held hands. As she listened to Mr. Allen's voice, the fear seemed to drain out of her with each word. "Lord," he prayed, "here we are in a heap of trouble. Our brakes are out, and there may be bandits in those trees over there waiting to attack us. But we know that we are in Your hands. We know that this whole trip is in Your hands.

We ask for Your protection right now, and we praise You for being the loving Dad that You are. We love You. In Jesus' name, Amen."

As soon as his prayer was over, Mr. Allen said quietly, "OK. Let's get back in the vehicles. We'll wait another few minutes to make sure the brakes have had plenty of time to cool, then we'll start down the mountain again."

Twenty minutes later when Mr. Allen pulled the pickup back out onto the road he checked the brakes. They gripped perfectly. All the way down the mountain, Tory prayed silently for the brakes to continue to hold. It wasn't until the road leveled out just before the Honduran border that Tory relaxed her prayer vigil and began to think about what lay ahead. She pulled out her journal and began to write.

What a day this has been! Surely nothing we have to face in Honduras could be as scary or nerve-wracking as today. Could it?

CHAPTER FOUR

Almost as if by magic the scenery changed again as the Honduran border came into view. The lush jungle gave way to a high desert landscape where rolling mountainsides sported tall, stately pines. Tory stuck her head out the window and breathed deeply of the fragrant air.

"This is *beautiful,*" she exclaimed over and over. "I didn't know Honduras was this pretty."

At the border, a tall, middle-aged man with a neat mustache and a handful of official papers stepped up to Mr. Allen's side of the pickup.

"I am Roberto Mendanez," the man said, smiling and extending his hand in greeting. "I have been waiting for you. Much of the paperwork is completed that will allow us to travel on to the orphanage. But there is more we will have to do now that you are here."

Tory had heard of Dr. Mendanez and knew he was a physician at the Santa Barbara hospital and a strong supporter of the orphanage there. She wanted to ask him questions about the medical work in Santa Barbara but decided to wait for better timing. The most important business now was to navigate the border crossing and get the trucks and the trailer full of supplies safely to the orphanage.

The last rays of the sun streaked lavender and gold across the western sky as Mr. Allen and Dr. Mendanez returned to the vehicles with the completed paperwork. Tory and Adam had spent the time waiting attempting to talk to the crowd of barefoot children that pressed in around them. Tory wondered where the children's parents were. No one seemed concerned that even the very smallest children spent hours at the border crossing.

"I have arranged rooms for us in the hotel here," Dr. Mendanez explained. "It is not really safe to travel at night. Bandits sometimes block the road with big rocks then attack travelers when they stop and get out to move the rocks."

Mr. Allen nodded. "I think that's wise, but we can camp in our vehicles. We won't go to the expense of a room. But let's find somewhere to eat some supper. Is anybody hungry?"

"Yes!" Tory and Adam chorused in unison. Tory glanced at Adam, embarrassed, but he just grinned and winked at her.

It took a few moments for Tory's eyes to adjust to the dim light in the restaurant. Small wooden tables and chairs were arranged cozily around the room. Melon-colored stucco walls cast a soft glow on the white tablecloths. A gallon jar in the center of each table held layers of red and white onions and peppers.

Mr. Allen and Adam pushed two of the small tables together in the center of the room so the group could sit together. Dr. Mendanez slipped onto the chair next to Mr. Allen and Linda and began an earnest conversation about the work of the orphanage. Adam sat down next to Tory. He reached for the jar of vegetables. "Want to take a culinary adventure?" he whispered to Tory, an impish look on his face as he took the lid from the jar and speared a forkful of onions.

"No. I don't think so," she whispered back. Something about the look on Adam's face set off a warning bell in her brain. "You go ahead, though. I'll watch."

Adam popped the forkful of pickled onions, carrots, and peppers into his mouth and chewed carefully, his face a mask of self-control. Not a flicker of reaction registered on his face. He speared another forkful and held it out to Tory.

"See? It's good." He waved the vegetables closer to her mouth. "You'll like it."

Tory sighed. "OK," she said, with an air of resignation. "If you insist. If I'm going to be a Honduran, I need to eat like one, I guess." She took the fork and gingerly nibbled at the onions. Then she just opened her mouth wide and ate the whole forkful.

As soon as she started chewing, searing heat ripped through her mouth like a forest fire. Hot tears slid down her cheeks, and she gasped for breath. When she opened her eyes, a pretty young Honduran girl with a white apron over her skirt and blouse stood beside the table. The girl suppressed a giggle with one hand and held out a glass of water with the other.

"Caliente," the girl said, still smiling as Tory gulped down the whole glass of water.

Adam reached over and patted Tory on the back. "It means 'hot,'" he announced solemnly. Tory glared at him.

"So what is the Spanish word for 'I'll never believe anything you say ever again'?"

The meal was simple fare but, as the fire in her mouth subsided, Tory found it very tasty. Fried bananas or *plátanos* served with seasoned black beans, a fresh salad, and tender tortillas made up the bulk of the meal.

"These bananas taste completely different when they're cooked," Tory mused, holding up a forkful of *plátanos* and studying it as if she were seeing the fruit in a whole new light.

Dr. Menandez laughed. "So I take it you were introduced to our *plátanos* in their raw state?" He shook his head. "It is important to remember in a different culture that things are not always as one might expect. One learns not to assume." He reached over and patted Tory on the back. "We're glad you're here, Tory. You'll do fine. It's just different here than in the U.S. You'll see when you visit the hospital." His voice trailed off, the last part of the sentence barely audible.

Tory put the forkful of *plátanos* down on her plate, a sinking feeling welling up in her stomach. There was something in Dr. Menandez' voice that frightened her. What would she find at the village hospital? All along she'd pictured a neat little block building with starched white curtains at the windows and rows of small cots. She didn't expect electric hospital beds and the newest medical equipment, just the basic blood pressure cuffs, thermometers, IV equipment, and bandaging supplies. How "different" could it really be?

"Dr. Menandez," she asked, suddenly feeling like a shy schoolgirl, "could you tell me about my duties in Santa Barbara? What will I be doing at the hospital?"

Dr. Menandez gave her a strange look, then cleared his throat. "Well, that's a fair question. I guess you would be interested in knowing ahead of time what to expect. You'll be working with the children, mostly. Adam will be going with you up into the villages to find the orphan children that are in need of a safe and nurturing environment. They have lots of medical needs, so your hands will be pretty full just with their care."

Tory felt the anxiety drain out of her as if someone

32

had pulled a plug deep inside where her deepest fears pooled. She loved the thought of working with children. She was sure she could handle anything if it involved a child. Especially if Adam was there with her. She sneaked a glance at him and saw that he was listening intently to Dr. Menandez.

It was still dark the next morning when Mr. Allen rapped on the window of the pickup. Tory groaned and turned over in her sleeping bag. She heard Mr. Allen call Adam from the sleeping berth he'd created on top of the boxes in the back of the Toyota.

After a quick breakfast of sliced mangoes and sweet bread, the group started on their journey to Santa Barbara. Dr. Menandez climbed into the pickup with the Allens, so Tory rode with Adam. They traveled south and west on a road so full of potholes that they couldn't drive more than 35 miles an hour. As the sky began to lighten behind them, Tory could see range after range of mountains, bathed in the golden pink of sunrise.

"Whew," she breathed. "It just keeps getting better, doesn't it?"

Adam nodded. "I don't think I've ever been anywhere prettier than Honduras." He looked at her with the same strange look that Dr. Menandez had the night before. "It has the most beautiful scenery and the most heartbreaking and tragic scenery. Are you up for seeing both?"

Tory gulped and nodded solemnly. "Yes, I think so," she said.

Suddenly, a thundering "boom" rocked the trailer in front of them and the pickup screeched to a stop. Adam slammed on his brakes to avoid a collision. The trailer sat tilted at a crazy angle, the right rear tire lying in shreds on the pavement. Dr. Menandez and Mr. Allen piled out of the pickup truck and walked around and around the truck and trailer, checking all the other tires and always ending up standing by the flat tire, shaking their heads in disbelief.

A rushing creek tumbled down the mountainside above the road where the tire had blown. It entered a culvert and flowed under the road. Tory followed Adam along the roadside to a faint path along a ridge that led to an outcropping of rocks. Perched beside Adam on the edge of the farthest rock, she could see where the water burst out of the culvert to plunge down the face of a rock cliff, a rainbow arching in its mist.

Tory let out a long breath. "I *have* to get my camera," she said. She started to get up.

"Wait, Tory," Adam said, touching her arm and pointing to a place in the air just above the falls. "Look."

A pair of brilliant blue butterflies danced above the falls, their delicate wings fluttering on the air currents like tiny ballerinas. They swooped and dived, as if playing a game of tag.

"It looks like they're hang gliding," Adam said, laughing out loud. "I'd like to be out there with them."

Tory stared at her hands as memories of Kane and the day he took her up in the airplane and flew over her parents' farm flooded her thoughts. She caught her breath as the feelings of loss over Kane's death hit her again, full force.

"Are you OK?" she heard Adam ask through the fog of pain. She shook her head slowly.

"No," she said. "A good friend of mine died not long ago. He was a pilot and talking about flying just reminded me of how much his death still hurts." Hot tears squeezed from her closed eyes and trickled down her cheeks. Adam slipped his arm around her and held her close as she cried.

"Here," he said, pressing a cloth hanky into her hand. "It's clean. Use it for as long as you need it."

Tory sat beside Adam, eyes shut, leaning against his shoulder and listening to the water until Mr. Allen called that the tire was fixed and they could move on. Adam helped her up.

"Are you OK now?" he asked, still holding her hand.

Tory sniffed and smiled up at him. "Yes," she said. "I'm OK." She gently withdrew her hand and started back up the trail toward the trucks. Then she stopped and turned to face Adam. "Hey, thanks for being there for me."

Adam grinned and Tory noticed that his eyes were as intense a blue as the butterflies' wings in the morning sun. He gave her a little bow. "My pleasure, madam. That's my job."

She turned away again, but glanced back over her shoulder just in time to see Adam's grin fade and a serious, thoughtful look take its place. There was something else in his expression, too; something she couldn't quite read. When he caught her eye, the look disappeared as quickly as it had come.

The hours passed as the little caravan bumped its way along the rutted, pothole-riddled road. Once a cow blocked the road and Mr. Allen jumped from the pickup and chased it into the nearby field. As the sun climbed high in the sky, the air grew hot. Tory unfolded Adam's hanky and wiped the grime from her face. Her hair hung in a dusty limp braid over her shoulder. Her only bath had been a quick sponging in the utility room of the hotel near the border.

Adam looked over at Tory as she sprinkled the hanky with water from her canteen and held it to her face.

"Yeah, I feel pretty grubby, too," he said.

"Wouldn't a shower feel great right now?"

Just then another "boom" rocked the cab and the trailer in front of them swerved from side to side. This time it was the left rear trailer tire that blew.

"Oh, no," Tory moaned. "Not another delay."

Adam pulled the Toyota to the side of the road and parked. As soon as Tory opened her door, she could hear the rush of water over rocks. Just past the place where they pulled over, another creek gushed down the hillside. She ran across the road to where the water flowed through the culvert under the road. The water spewing out of the opening fell about 30 feet to a turquoise pool lined with boulders.

Tory sprinted back to the little silver truck and grabbed her backpack from the cab. Rummaging through her toiletries she pulled out a travel-sized bottle of shampoo and a bar of soap and held them up triumphantly. "Guess what, Adam," she announced. "I'm going to have that shower after all!"

Adam followed her, a puzzled look on his face until he saw the waterfall and the pool. "Oh, this is just too good to be true," he shouted.

Tory gasped as she plunged, clothes and all, into the icy water of the pool. Adam stood on the bank, watching her. "How is it?" he called.

"Great. Feels good."

Adam leaped into the pool, disappearing under the water, then surfacing with a screech of surprise. "Whoa, this is *cold*."

Tory grinned wickedly. "But it's an *adventure*, don't you think?"

Swimming to where the waterfall hit the pool, she shampooed her hair quickly and rinsed it under the cascade of bone-chilling water. The droplets pounded her head like little jack hammers, but it felt so good to be clean she didn't even care.

"Hey, can I borrow some of that?" Adam held his hands up for Tory to throw him the shampoo. As she tossed the little bottle to him, Tory noticed the goose-bumps all over Adam's chest and arms and the deepening blue tinge to his lips.

"What is the Spanish word for 'cold'?" she asked.

"Frio."

"Well, I think this water is *muy frio,* and I'm getting out before hypothermia sets in." Tory plunged under the waterfall to make sure she'd gotten all the shampoo rinsed from her hair, then swam to the rock-piled shore. Adam followed close behind her.

The three adults stood at the edge of the bank as Tory and Adam climbed back up to the road, their clothes and hair dripping. Mr. Allen shook his head in bewilderment at the sight. "Crazy kids," he muttered under his breath. Dr. Menandez just laughed.

Linda handed them each a towel. "You two had better get dried off. It's still a long drive to Santa Barbara."

Turning to follow her husband to the truck, she smiled. "It looked great," she whispered. "I should have joined you."

"Yep," Adam said, winking at Tory, "it was definitely an *adventure.* And something tells me there are many more to come."

CHAPTER FIVE

The last glow of twilight was just fading as the trucks pulled into the driveway of the orphanage in Santa Barbara. Tory jumped out of the Toyota as soon as it stopped rolling, eager to move around after so many hours of sitting in the cramped cab. She looked around at the buildings, surprised that she could barely make out their shapes in the gathering darkness.

"Where are the children?" she asked Dr. Menandez, puzzled at the silence of the place. "Why aren't there any lights on anywhere?"

Dr. Menandez smiled at her eagerness. "The children aren't here yet," he said. "We have some construction details to complete before we can bring them." He pointed up the drive to what appeared to be a fairly large house. "This is the director's home. This is where you and Adam will stay with the Allens. Let's go on in. It has electricity, but we need to turn it on. We won't have water in the house for a few more days, though."

Tory's heart sank as she thought of going for several days without a shower. She already felt dusty and dirty again. She followed Mr. Allen and Dr. Menandez up the sidewalk to the house. Just as she reached the porch, a wizened little man, his shoulders stooped with age, stepped out in front of her holding a lantern. A tiny wrinkled woman stood beside him clutching a ragged shawl to her shoulders. The man held out an orange and said something in very rapid Spanish. The old woman nodded and beamed at Tory, obviously pleased with what her husband was saying.

"I-I can't understand you," Tory stammered. She took the orange that the man offered, hoping that he wasn't expecting a trade for something. She did a quick mental inventory of all the customs she had learned about the people in this area, trying to remember the social protocol when it came to gift giving.

"He's offering it to you as a gift," she heard Adam whisper from somewhere just behind her. "It's OK just to take it. These are very hospitable people. Just say 'gracias.' That's Spanish for 'thank you.'"

Tory smiled. "Gracias," she said. She pointed to herself. "I'm Tory."

The old man's face lit up in a huge toothless grin. "Don Victor," he said proudly, jabbing a crooked finger toward his own chest. Then he grabbed his wife's arm and pulled her forward. "Doña Chila."

It was impossible to tell the woman's age, but Tory felt sure she had never seen a human being with so many wrinkles. Doña Chila looked down at her weathered hands, shy in the presence of strangers. Tory reached out and placed her hand on the woman's shoulder.

"I'm so glad to meet you," she said, knowing the woman could not understand. She hoped her tone would convey acceptance and welcome even if she couldn't say the words.

Adam stepped forward just then and extended his hand to Don Victor, speaking to him in Spanish. Don Victor nodded his head vigorously and began an avalanche of Spanish words. Tory watched, amazed.

"What is he saying?" she asked, at the first brief pause in the conversation. "How can you understand him? He talks so fast."

Adam laughed. "No faster than *you* talk. It just sounds fast because you're unfamiliar with the language. You'll catch on quicker than you think. You'll see."

Don Victor studied Adam's face as he answered Tory. Even Doña Chila lifted her eyes and watched them, as if trying to absorb the unfamiliar words.

"See?" Adam said. "Our language sounds just as strange to them. And, by the way, he was telling me that he and his wife live here and that she will make tortillas for us on her *comal* every day."

Tory looked around the yard, surprised. The lantern light cast long eery shadows from the nearby shrubs and trees. "How can they live here? Where?"

"Probably in a shack behind the house," Adam said soberly. "They're probably very poor. I doubt their accommodations are very fancy. We'll have to pay them a visit in the morning."

Even before Adam finished speaking, the old couple disappeared into the night. "I'm surprised they came out after dark at all." He heaved the suitcase he'd been carrying up onto the porch. "There is a lot of superstition among the older people. They believe that demons in the form of dogs, cats, pigs, and chickens roam the night just waiting to devour some poor person."

Tory shivered and glanced into the darkness. A tiny speck of light danced just beyond the sidewalk. Suddenly it was joined by two more flickering lights. Then thousands of lights filled the yard.

"Look, Adam," she squealed. "Fireflies!" She ran out into the yard, and Adam joined her, chasing the shimmering insects around and around until they both collapsed on the grass in exhaustion.

"I hope you're saving some of that energy for unloading these trucks," Mr. Allen called from the porch. He hung a Coleman lantern on a hook on one of the porch crossbeams. "Don't you kids want to see your rooms? I think Dr. Menandez has the electricity on now."

The house, a white stucco structure with cement roof and floors, was simple but functional, with four fair-sized bedrooms, a living room area, a large kitchen, and a bathroom. The living room and kitchen were empty of furniture. Tory walked through them and down the long hall to her room. A bare lightbulb hung from the ceiling.

A cockroach skittered across the floor as Tory pulled the string to turn on the light. She took off her shoe and threw it at the intruder, shuddering at the thought of sharing her room with the creepy insects. Her furniture consisted of a small cot and a wooden crate lying on its side to serve as a bedside stand. She pulled a colorful scarf and a candle from her backpack and arranged them on the crate.

"Staking your claim?" Tory looked up to see Adam grinning at her. "Come see my digs."

Rows of shelves covered one whole wall of Adam's room. Clothes and shoes in all sizes, obviously meant for distribution, lined the shelves. A mat on the floor served as a bed. The room had no dresser or bedside stand. Adam's suitcase lay on the floor in the corner, its contents neatly arranged as if in a dresser drawer.

"There you go," Adam said, a pleased tone in his voice. "I'm settled in already."

Tory stared around the room. "But there isn't anything in here! Don't you have a bed?"

"Nah. I don't need one. I sleep just fine on the floor." Adam squatted down and patted the bedroll on the floor for emphasis.

Shaking her head, Tory backed out of the room and headed down the hall to help unload the trucks. Adam followed close behind. Within an hour, all the contents of both trucks and the trailer lay in heaps on the living room floor. Linda sat down on a 100-pound burlap bag full of red beans.

"Now to get it all put away," she said with a heavy sigh.

Dr. Menandez emerged from the kitchen, where he'd carried a box full of utensils and pots and pans. "Oh, I forgot to tell you," he said, embarrassed. "We have an all night prayer vigil at the church tonight. The people want to meet you. It starts in an hour." He turned to Adam and Tory. "Could you sing a song for us?"

"S-sure," Adam said, glancing at Tory with question marks in his eyes. "I'd be up for it. How about you?"

Tory gulped. She liked to sing, but not usually up front and definitely not in front of a church full of perfect strangers from another culture. The old feeling of fear started to wash over her like stagnant pond water.

Father, I came here to serve You, she prayed silently. *I give this fear to You and refuse to let it rule my decisions.*

"Yes," she said at last, feeling a surge of strength and confidence that she knew had to have come from God. "Yes, I'll be glad to sing for the meeting."

Mr. Allen produced an old guitar and Adam stepped out onto the front porch and began tuning it and practicing chords. Tory watched the dancing fireflies as she listened to his strumming. Finally, he said, "OK, I'm ready. Let's try 'Seek Ye First.'"

Adam's clear strong harmony blended perfectly with her soprano as they sang the old familiar words. Finishing the song, they sat staring into the inky darkness. Adam broke the stillness. "It sounds different here, somehow," he said thoughtfully. "The words mean more."

Tory thought of the terrifying ride down the mountain in Guatemala when the brakes went out on the truck and the fear she'd felt at the threat of ambush. And now, in this new place with so many uncertainties ahead, she sensed the beginning of a different kind of trust in God. Deeper. More urgent. More real.

"Yes," she said quietly. "I think I know what you mean."

The little church was packed by the time Tory, Adam, and the Allens arrived. Throngs of children, their bright faces beaming a welcome to the newcomers, piled out through the door to greet them. Tory hugged several of the smaller children who ran to her with open arms. A little boy took her hand shyly and led her to the front of the church. She sat on the rough hand-hewn wooden bench and gazed around in wonder.

Open screenless windows lined both sides of the church. The floor was concrete. A simple wooden pulpit stood at the front on a raised wooden platform large enough to hold eight to 10 people. Everywhere she looked, people chattered excitedly—young mothers with babies in their arms, older men in threadbare but neatly pressed suits, teenagers dressed in the latest style. And the children, always barefoot, with huge brown eyes that seemed to reach right inside her and pull on every heartstring she had.

Adam made his way across the crowded room toward her, a young Honduran man at his heels.

"Tory, this is Antonio," Adam said, as he slid onto the bench beside her. "His wife and children aren't here yet, but they will be soon."

Antonio extended his hand in greeting, and Tory shook it. It was a warm, friendly handshake, and Tory found herself liking this bright young man immediately.

"Welcome," Antonio said. "My English is bad, but I want you to know we are glad you are here."

"No," Tory exclaimed. "Your English is *good*. Much better than my Spanish. But it will get better, I hope."

Antonio smiled. "You will learn quickly. You will see."

"I think so, too," Adam said, nodding his encouragement. "And I'll help you learn. I'll sit by you and translate the service for you if you want me to. That way you can start to pick up the patterns of the words."

A beautiful young woman with three boys in tow suddenly appeared next to Antonio and stood shyly, waiting for him to acknowledge her. A look of pride spread across Antonio's face as he took the woman's hand and held it out to Tory. "I would like you to meet my wife, Christina," he said. "She does not speak English."

"Buenas," Tory said, trying to remember the correct words to speak when you meet someone new. She shook Christina's hand. Christina gently nudged the oldest boy forward as Antonio introduced him as Dario. The youngest was named Josue. Ramon, the 10-year-old, grinned mischievously at Adam and pulled a green lizard from his pocket. Holding it out at arm's length, he offered the lizard to Tory.

"Thank you, I mean *gracias,"* Tory said. She took the lizard and held it gently in her palm, stroking the leathery skin on its sides. Adam stared at her in surprise. She just smiled at him as she handed the lizard back to the boy.

Tory was surprised at how much she enjoyed the song service even though she couldn't understand the words. The tunes sounded familiar and the worshipful spirit didn't require language to be understood. When Adam and Tory stood to sing their song, a quiet hush fell over the group. Tory saw tears in many of the people's eyes as they listened. Few of them understood English, she knew, but they heard the message of the song anyway.

When the pastor began to speak, Adam sat close beside Tory and whispered the English translation into her ear. The pastor talked about the importance of being friends with God and trusting Him no matter what happens. Adam tried to keep up with him in the translation, but sometimes picked out only a word here and there. Still, Tory found it surprisingly easy to follow the idea of the sermon. She listened to the pastor's words, then to Adam's translation and strained her mind to detect some kind of pattern, some connection between the two.

By the end of the sermon, she felt exhausted. She knew from Adam's translation of the announcements that many of the church members were staying up all night at the church to pray for their loved ones and neighbors and for evangelism in their hard to reach area, but she was glad the pastor had urged them to rest from their arduous trip.

"I need the gift of languages," she told Adam wearily as they headed for the pickup after the service.

Adam laughed. "You and me both. I didn't realize translating was so hard. You have to actively think in two languages at the same time."

When they arrived back at the orphanage, Tory changed from her dress into a pair of jeans. Adam disappeared into his room. The Allens hadn't returned from the meeting yet and Tory suspected that they would stay and talk to the pastor for quite some time.

She pulled a flashlight from her backpack and started for the door.

"Hey, where do you think you're going without me?"

She jumped at the sound of Adam's voice. "I have something I want to check out," she said. "I thought you were asleep already."

Adam held up his own flashlight. "Are you kidding? And let you keep the adventure to yourself? Not a chance."

Bright stars dotted the night sky as Tory picked her way down a path around the house and back into the field behind it.

"Do you know where you're going?" Adam asked, shining his flashlight around at the trees and bushes beside the path.

"I know what I'm looking for, if that's what you mean."

A loud snort sounded from just beyond the fence they'd been following. Tory stopped dead in her tracks. Then she turned off her flashlight and cautiously moved forward, talking softly into the darkness.

"It's just me. I won't hurt you. Come on over to the fence, little one." She reached into her jeans pocket and pulled out a piece of dried apple that she'd filched from the kitchen on her way out. She moved close to the fence and held the apple out in her flattened palm. Adam's flashlight beam moved closer until he was standing right beside her.

Adam turned off his light. "I should have known you couldn't wait until morning to see this guy," he said softly. "Do you really think he'll come over here to greet two perfect strangers in the dark? For all he knows, we might be planning to eat him."

"He'll come," Tory said. "He's as curious about us as we are about him. Besides, he smells the apple."

Tory could hear the soft thud of unshod hooves in

the grass. A few seconds later, a warm muzzle pushed against her palm, lipping the apples and snorting softly. She strained to see the horse in the darkness, but she didn't turn on her flashlight, afraid the light would frighten him. Smoothing the fur along his well-muscled neck, she followed the arch of his crest with her hand.

"Hey, you are a much bigger boy than I thought you'd be," she whispered, surprised at the horse's height. "The other horses I saw on the way here were much smaller." She pulled another piece of apple from her pocket and offered it to him. He nibbled at the edge of the apple, then greedily gobbled it up.

Adam moved in close beside Tory and extended his hand. He reached under the horse's chin and started scratching.

Tory whistled in surprise at the ease with which he moved. "You've been around horses before, haven't you?"

"Yep," Adam said.

"Why didn't you tell me?"

"You never asked."

Tory couldn't see Adam's face, but she knew he was smiling, feeling he had pulled one over on her. She patted the horse a final time and moved back from the fence. "We'll see you tomorrow, big boy. Then we'll see who *really* knows how to ride."

CHAPTER SIX

The grass in the yard felt moist to Tory's feet as she stepped outside to breathe the early morning air. She'd heard Mr. Allen say that the rainy season in this part of Honduras was just ending, so she supposed a gentle rain must have fallen during the night. The house and yard looked completely different in the daytime.

Tall ironwood trees lined the cement walk that stretched from the road to the front porch. In one spot, a tree root stuck out from under the sidewalk, cracking the cement. The house's white stucco walls glowed almost pink in the early light.

Walking around the side of the house, Tory spotted a tiny hut built of old lumber and sheets of corrugated metal leaning haphazardly against the back of the house. A large clay oven stood beside the hut. A sheet of metal resting over a bed of coals on the top and an opening in the front seemed to be its main baking compartment. Doña Chila stood beside the clay stove, patting out tortillas with her weathered old hands.

"Buenos dias," Tory called out. Doña Chila looked up from the *comal* and flashed a toothless smile. She began to talk in Spanish, holding a plateful of steaming tortillas out to Tory. Tory took two and handed the plate back to her. *"Gracias,"* she said, suddenly realizing that her stomach was rumbling with hunger.

A black and white speckled hen with eight fluffy

chicks pecked at the ground around the old woman's feet. Doña Chila crumbled one of the tortillas and tossed the pieces in front of the hen. The hen clucked softly to her babies and picked at the crumbs with her sharp beak. The chicks quickly followed her example.

Tory nibbled at the edge of one of the tortillas. It was tender and flaky and tasted like a corn chip, only better. "M-mm-m," she said, taking a larger bite. She circled her hand on her middle to show that she liked it. Doña Chila nodded and smiled. *"Que bueno,"* she said, handing Tory another hot tortilla.

Just then Adam appeared around the corner of the house, his dark hair tousled as if he'd just crawled out of bed. "Hey, where's mine?" he asked cheerfully. He rattled off a string of Spanish words to Doña Chila and she laughed heartily and handed him the filled plate.

Adam wiggled his eyebrows at Tory. "It pays to get in good with the cook," he said. He grabbed three tortillas from the top of the stack and devoured them. Then he asked Doña Chila a question in Spanish. She pointed to the field behind the house and talked excitedly, waving her arms and shaking her head.

Tory looked back and forth from Doña Chila's animated face to Adam's thoughtful one. Adam asked the old woman another question and this time, instead of answering it, Doña Chila marched to a shed at the edge of the backyard and disappeared inside. When she came out she held a leather bridle. She thrust it into Adam's hands, still shaking her head and fussing in Spanish.

"Come on, Tory," Adam chuckled. He held up the bridle and headed for the pasture. "It's time to meet Tamarindo in the daylight."

Tory jogged to catch up with Adam. "Who is Tamarindo?" she puffed. "And what was *that* all about?"

Reaching the fence at the edge of the pasture, Tory gasped in amazement. There, in a field dotted with tiny yellow flowers, stood a magnificent chocolate brown gelding. Even from a distance, it was clear that this was no ordinary horse. He moved toward them, his muscles rippling under his shiny dark coat.

"That," Adam announced, "is Tamarindo."

Tory let out a long, low whistle. "Whew. I didn't expect him to be so beautiful."

She held out her hand as Tamarindo approached the fence, allowing him to sniff her. She kept her eyes fixed down and a little to the side with a slight turn of her shoulders to portray a non-threatening posture to the horse.

The horse nickered softly and nuzzled her hand. Tory reached up with her palm flat and rubbed Tamarindo's dark face. "Look, Adam," she whispered. "He doesn't have a speck of white on him anywhere. He's incredible."

"It's amazing how he's responding to you. Doña Chila said he's wild and out of control. No one here will ride him."

Tory laughed. "So that's what she was so fired up about. I wondered. Did she say how Tamarindo got his name?"

"He is almost the color of the paste of the tamarindo pod, inside the pod and around its seed. The pods grow on trees around here. The paste is very dark brown." Adam made a face. "And it's *sour*. That is, until you dilute it with water and sweeten it. Then it's the best fruit drink on the planet. It's my favorite."

Tamarindo pushed Tory's shoulder with his nose as if looking for a treat. "You remember the apples from last night, don't you boy," she said, reaching into her jeans pocket. She pulled out several slices of apple and held them out to the horse. Then she slipped between the wires of the fence and ran her hand along Tamarindo's neck. "Adam, hand me the bridle," she said evenly. "I'm going to try to put it on him."

"Are you nuts?" Adam shook his head. "We don't even know this horse. Why don't you let me try first."

Adam held the bridle out, but before Tory could reach for it, Tamarindo wheeled and bolted to the other side of the pasture. As soon as he reached a safe distance, he stopped and turned toward them, watching their every move.

"I don't think he's had very good handling," Tory said, trying to hide the disappointment she felt. "It may take some work to win his trust."

Suddenly Adam brightened. "Wait a minute," he said. "Let me try something else. I read a book a few weeks ago about this man who works with horses using their own body language. Did you see how Tamarindo ran just a certain distance away and then stopped and looked to see if we were chasing him? That's the 'flight instinct' that all herd animals use. He doesn't have any intention of running and running. He just wants to run a safe distance from us and rest."

"So what does that have to do with winning his trust?"

"Everything." Adam climbed through the fence and stood beside Tory in the pasture. "According to that trainer, horses establish a 'pecking order' in their herds. If I can convince Tamarindo through my body language that I'm the dominant herd member, he will not only trust me, he'll do anything I want!"

"Whoa." Tory plopped to the ground, careful to avoid sitting on an anthill. "You go, guy. This I've got to see."

Tory watched intently as Adam, swinging the reins of the bridle forward in a circular motion, approached the wary horse. As soon as Adam got close enough to touch the reins to Tamarindo's hindquarters, the gelding trotted away. Adam followed patiently, still swinging the reins. As long as the horse retreated, he kept advancing, his eyes locked with the horse's and his shoulders squared in an aggressive stance.

"Watch his inside ear," Adam called softly to Tory. "That's the one he's listening to me with. The other one is listening to everything else. Watch that ear stop moving as his head goes down and tips toward me. He wants to stop all this running around. He's just about ready to decide I'm the boss."

Tamarindo slowed to a walk, his head almost touching the ground. Sure enough, the ear closest to Adam stopped flicking back and forth and pointed directly toward him. The horse's mouth opened and he began chomping and sticking his tongue out in much the same subordinate gesture that Tory had seen young colts use in the presence of older, more dominant horses.

As Tamarindo demonstrated his submissiveness, Adam abruptly assumed a submissive stance, too. He lowered his eyes and turned away from the horse, standing quietly in the middle of the field. Tamarindo moved toward him and stood beside him, as docile as a kitten. Adam, keeping his eyes averted, reached up and rubbed the gelding's forehead. Then he walked away, with the horse following behind him as he walked in large circles in the field.

Tory stood up, staring in disbelief. "How did you get him to do that?" she asked in amazement. "He acts like you hypnotized him."

Adam laughed. "I just talked horse language to him and now he thinks I'm the boss. Now I'll bet we can get that bridle on."

Tamarindo stood still and accepted the bit without any problems. He even lowered his head so Adam could slip the headstall of the bridle up over his ears. All the while he worked, Adam kept up a calm, even flow of words. Tory knew he was using his voice to comfort the horse and maintain the level of confidence he'd achieved with him in the field.

"Ready to go for a ride?" Adam asked, grinning triumphantly. He gathered the reins at Tamarindo's withers and speaking gently to the horse, moved to his side and vaulted up onto his back.

Tamarindo quivered, his legs bunched together as if he were ready to buck. Tory held her breath, waiting for the horse to explode. Adam reached down and ran his hand along the side of the horse's neck. "It's all right, boy. We're going to do this together. You'll be OK. You can trust me. I'm the boss, remember?"

Gradually, the gelding calmed. His head went down and he heaved a sigh of submission. Adam squeezed the horse's sides with his lower legs, clucking softly, and loosening the reins slightly. Tamarindo stepped out, gingerly at first, then with increased confidence. Adam reined him in a figure eight and several large circles. Then he pulled the horse to a stop beside Tory.

"I think he's ready," Adam said. "Want to hop on with me and let's do a little exploring?"

Tory's eyes opened wide in surprise. "Double? Are you kidding?"

"No. He'll do fine." Adam reached back and patted the spot on Tamarindo's back just behind where he sat. "Come on, I'll help you up." He held out his left hand for Tory to grab. She reached out and grasped it and sprang up in a belly flop behind Adam. Tamarindo began to quiver again, but Adam talked soothingly to him until Tory got her legs straightened around.

"It's OK, boy," Adam crooned. "You'll have to get used to this arrangement because the three of us are going to be spending a lot of time together. You're going to be our main mode of transportation."

Once Tory got herself comfortably positioned Adam clucked to the horse again. "Let's go, Tamarindo." The gelding stepped out without hesitation and walked along the path toward the pasture gate, obeying Adam's leg aides and gentle tugs of the reins.

Tory felt herself relaxing more and more as it became clear that Tamarindo had fully accepted Adam's authority and had no intention of rebelling. "Dare we say this is a miracle?" she whispered to Adam, letting herself sway with the rhythm of the horse's smooth gait.

Adam chuckled. "He is doing remarkably well, isn't he? I agree that he's probably had some mishandling in the past. But somewhere in his early years he had some excellent training. The misbehavior was a bluff, I suspect. Fear can do funny things."

"Hm-m-m," Tory murmured. "Yes. I suppose it can."

A rough dirt road ran parallel to the main highway beyond the pasture gate. Adam neck reined Tamarindo to the northeast. The road was dotted with cow pies. Obviously this route was popular among the cattle drivers that moved their herds from place to place, trying to find enough grass for them on the barren hillsides.

About a mile from the house the road dipped down toward a clear, fast-flowing river. An old stone bridge, cloaked in hanging foliage, spanned the river, its ancient arches pocked from the battering of a thousand floods. Just past the bridge, the water cascaded over a cement buttress into a broad pool.

The sun had already begun climbing and Tory felt a

band of sweat beading up on her forehead. She wiped it off with the sleeve of her T-shirt. She could feel the sweat from Tamarindo's back soaking into her jeans.

Adam glanced back at her. "Hot, isn't it?" He pointed to the river, grinning. "What is it about this country? It seems that just when you need a nice cold river, there it is!" He reined Tamarindo in beside an ironwood tree about 30 feet from the riverbank and motioned for Tory to slip down.

Adam tethered Tamarindo to one of the lower branches of the tree and followed Tory to the riverbank. Before she could blink twice, he pulled off his shoes and shirt and dived into the clear water.

"Woo-hoo," he yelled when he surfaced. "We've found our swimming hole! Who cares if we ever get water in the house. This is the world's best bathtub."

Tory stood on a rock at the edge of the water, poised to dive, when she glanced up at the bridge above them. There from the shadows of the overhanging branches, she saw a man staring at her, his dark face twisted into a lewd sneer. She opened her mouth but no sound came out. Heart pounding, she searched the water for Adam. When she looked back to where she'd seen the man, he was gone.

Suddenly Adam surfaced, just a few feet from the rock where she stood. He stared at Tory in surprise. "Hey, what's wrong? You're as white as a sheet. Did you see a ghost?"

"I-I don't know," Tory stammered, sinking down on the rock, her heart still beating wildly. "I saw a man among the trees. He was watching me with a really scary look on his face."

Adam pulled himself up on the rock, water streaming from his hair. Concern clouded his blue eyes. "Let's get out of here," he said, grabbing his shirt and pulling it on without even bothering to dry off.

Tamarindo stood quietly while Adam vaulted to his back and helped Tory up behind him. Adam urged the horse into a canter as he scrambled up the bank to the road. Tory glanced back at the row of trees that obscured the old bridge just as the slight form of a man stepped from the shadows, the sunlight glinting off something shiny in his hand.

CHAPTER SEVEN

M r. Allen stood on the porch watching as Adam and Tory galloped Tamarindo toward the house from the old livestock road. Adam let Tory off at the end of the sidewalk and took Tamarindo to the pasture to cool him down.

"What's the big hurry?" Mr. Allen asked as Tory walked stiffly up the sidewalk. "You guys act as if the devil's chasing you."

Tory shuddered, recalling the cold, evil look on the strange man's face. "We saw someone down at the river," she blurted. "The way he looked at me gave me the chills."

Mr. Allen's forehead wrinkled as he listened to Tory's description, and he rubbed his chin thoughtfully. "That doesn't sound good. I don't like the idea of you being followed like that. Don't ever go far from the house here without Adam or one of the other men. OK?"

Tory grimaced. "That's an easy promise to make."

Mr. Allen glanced around as if suddenly remembering something. "Where did Adam take the horse? I need you two to ride into town and check on some orphans."

"Sure thing," Tory said, swiping her hand across the back of her jeans. "But are you sure you want us to go looking like this?"

Just then Antonio drove up in the Ford pick-up. He screeched to a stop, jumped out of the truck, and hoisted an old western saddle and a wool saddle blanket from the back. He flashed a smile at Tory as he set them on the ground at her feet and she was struck with the sense of dignity and poise that surrounded him.

"Go ahead and get cleaned up," Mr. Allen told Tory after he thanked Antonio for getting the saddle. "This should keep you from getting quite as dirty as you ride. May be a little more comfortable, too."

Tory started across the yard to find Adam, but found him sauntering around the corner of the house with Tamarindo in tow. He grinned at her as he saw the saddle on the ground. "I take it this means our riding day is just beginning?"

Mr. Allen nodded. "There's a little girl in the hospital that I need for you to check on. You may have to go to her home village and assess her home situation. The road's too steep for the truck and besides, Antonio and I need to take it to the city to find some furniture for the house."

Antonio and Mr. Allen unloaded several five-gallon containers of water from the back of the truck while Adam saddled Tamarindo. They lined the plastic containers up on the kitchen counter for use as drinking water. Water for bathing and laundry would come from the river. Glancing down at her filthy jeans, Tory realized that she hadn't seen a washing machine anywhere. She thought of the woman she'd seen in Mexico scrubbing her laundry on a rock in the river. *Is that how I'm going to have to wash my clothes?*

She felt a light touch on her shoulder and turned to see Doña Chila at her side, beckoning her to follow. The old woman scurried around the house and led Tory to a cement structure that looked like an old stone countertop and sink. Thin metal bars were embedded in the top of the cement, lined up side by side to create a washboard. A huge bar of yellow soap perched on the edge of the sink.

Doña Chila held up a man's shirt stained with perspiration and dirt, and flopped it down on the washboard. Then she hoisted a bucket of river water and doused the shirt thoroughly. As soon as the shirt was wet enough to suit her, she swiped the bar of soap over it, back and forth several times. She scrubbed the shirt on the metal bars with both hands grinning triumphantly at Tory all the while. Finally, she placed the sodden shirt in the sink and doused it again, rinsing the soap away.

With a quick snap of the wrist, Doña Chila whisked the extra water from the shirt and hung it on the clothesline that ran from her little shanty to a tree behind the house. Then she pointed to Tory's jeans, telling her something in Spanish.

Tory shook her head and backed away. "I-I can't take them off here," she said, wishing for all the world that Adam would appear just now to help her explain. *"Un momento,"* she said, holding up one finger to show that she just needed one minute. She ran into the house and down to her room. She traded her sweat-stained jeans with another, cleaner pair and took the dirty ones outside to Doña Chila.

As she handed the jeans to the old woman she shook her head and pointed to Tory. She picked up the big yellow bar of soap and placed it in Tory's hand. "Oh, I see," Tory said, laughing. "You want *me* to learn how. Well, I think you've given me a great demonstration. Let's see how I do."

Tory poured water from the bucket over the jeans and swiped the soap across them as Doña Chila had done, then she scrubbed them on the metal bars. She was surprised at how effective the simple scrub board really was. The dirty spot on the jeans rubbed right out. Doña Chila stood by nodding her approval, her face smiling into a thousand tiny wrinkles. A few dousings of rinse water and the jeans looked clean and ready to hang out to dry.

"Great job."

Startled, Tory looked up to see Adam, seated on a saddled Tamarindo. The horse snorted and pawed the ground, chest muscles rippling with the movement. Adam had changed into fresh jeans and a bright blue shirt that just matched the shade of his eyes. Tory found herself staring at the striking pair.

Adam nudged Tamarindo a little closer. "Hey, we'd better head out," he said. "We have a lot of ground to cover before dark. Are you ready?"

"Uh, sure," Tory stammered, trying to regain her composure. "Let me hang these up and we can hit the trail."

The sun beat down on Tory's back as she rode behind Adam along the animal trail that paralleled the road to Santa Barbara. Tamarindo picked his way along the path, his ears flipping forward and back, listening to every new sound. He walked with a jaunty prance and an arched neck that Tory found amusing.

"This horse has quite the self-concept," she joked to Adam. "Especially if he can walk like this in this heat." She wiped the perspiration from her forehead. Tamarindo seemed to sense that she was talking about him and picked up his pace.

The animal trail faded out after they'd gone about two miles and Adam reined Tamarindo up onto the roadside. Tory glanced back to see a huge bus barreling down on them from behind. She tightened her grip on

Adam and held her breath as it whooshed past. The horse trembled and half crouched as the bus sped by, but stayed relatively calm.

"Phew," Tory breathed in relief. "I thought we were goners. This guy really trusts you, doesn't he?"

Adam just laughed. "Yep," was all he said in reply.

The hospital squatted on a dirt lot at the edge of town, its pink stucco walls flaking and falling away in chunks. Everywhere she looked, Tory saw people standing, sitting, or lying down in whatever shade they could find. Barefoot children ran in and out of the hospital doorway.

Adam guided Tamarindo carefully through the mass of people to a hitching post. Tory dismounted and tried to stand up, but her legs buckled under her, cramping from the long ride. Instantly she was deluged with children, all chattering in Spanish. Adam spoke a stern word in Spanish and the children scattered. Then he held out a hand and helped Tory to her feet.

"You OK?" he asked, concerned. "I guess we should have stopped halfway and exercised a little. I forgot how hours of nonstop riding can affect the circulation."

Tory smiled. "I'm fine," she said, walking in a little circle to stretch her calf muscles. "Let's go in and see if we can find the little girl Mr. Allen told us about."

The dingy hospital hallways were lined with people lounging about. Tory couldn't help but notice the open screenless windows with flies buzzing in and out. The hospital staff wore white uniforms and ran up and down the halls in a valiant attempt to care for the huge number of sick and injured, but it was clear that there could be no humanly possible way for such a small number of staff to care for so many.

Adam stopped one of the nurses and asked her a

question. She pointed to a room across the hall from where they stood. Tory followed Adam into the room. There on a dingy cot lay a tiny child with arms and legs as thin as two of Tory's fingers. Her huge stomach protruded from under a thin, dirty T-shirt. The diaper covering her bottom looked like it would fit a newborn.

The nurse, a young woman with jet black hair pulled back into a neat bun, stepped into the room behind them, carrying a baby bottle. She handed the bottle to Tory and said something in Spanish.

"She wants you to feed her," Adam explained.

Tory took the bottle and sat down on the cot next to the tiny girl. She scooped her up into her lap, careful to support her wobbling neck and poked the nipple of the bottle into her mouth. As the girl opened her mouth, Tory was shocked to see a full set of primary teeth. "Ask that nurse how old this child is!" she told Adam.

Adam spoke to the nurse and listened carefully as the young woman talked. After a long explanation, he turned to Tory. "They think she's 5 years old," he said, tears welling up in his eyes. "Her name is Yeny, which is the same as Jenny in English. This is her fifth or sixth hospitalization. Her mother is a prostitute and a beggar in one of the mountain villages. She has several other children. She purposely blinded one because she can get more money begging if she can elicit sympathy from people with her blind child.

"The reason Jenny is so emaciated is that her mom eats all the food she gets and doesn't give any of it to her. Even here in the hospital, the staff have to watch constantly because the mom will drink Jenny's bottle and eat any food that is brought in for her."

Tory swallowed hard, blinking back her own tears. She looked down at the helpless little girl, sucking with all her limited strength at the bottle of formula. Her huge dark eyes locked onto Tory's and a fierce determination to do whatever she could to save Jenny welled up in Tory's heart. She glanced up at Adam and saw the same look of resolve in his face.

"We have to leave her here until she gains some strength," Adam said quietly. "But we can come every day and make sure she's eating. The danger is that as soon as she's strong enough, the mom will try to take her back to her village. None of the staff here wants that to happen. It would mean certain death. We have to meet the mom and get her to promise that she'll let Jenny come to the orphanage."

The path up to the remote village where Jenny's mother lived wound past mountainside coffee plantations, through thick forest, and along a rushing mountain stream. Tamarindo never slackened his pace as he picked his way up the trail, carefully avoiding rocks and deep ruts in the road.

"This horse has more heart than anyone I've ever met," Tory said, shaking her head and shifting her position behind the saddle. "He doesn't even hesitate to do whatever we ask of him."

Adam nodded. "I'm pretty impressed with him, too. We've really given him a workout today, and he just looks around as he walks along as if we were on a sightseeing adventure just for him."

Tory laughed. "A horse that likes adventure. He fits right in."

They rounded a bend in the trail and there, clustered in an open meadow area, lay Jenny's village. Ragged scrawny chickens pecked at the bare ground and a black and white spotted goat pulled at a tattered piece of laundry hanging from a clothesline.

Cement block houses with tin roofs made up most of the village, with a few wooden lean-to shanties here and there. Adam asked an old man resting under a tree in the middle of the village where he could find Jenny's mother. The man pointed to one of the lean-to buildings.

Tethering Tamarindo to a tree, Adam made his way to the house. Tory followed close behind. There was no answer when they knocked at the makeshift door, but Tory heard a baby wailing inside. Adam knocked more insistently and the door swung open.

Jenny's mother stood in the doorway and stared at them, as if unable to comprehend that Americans would venture all the way up the mountain to her village. When Adam spoke to her in Spanish, she blinked in surprise, then stepped back and gestured for them to enter.

"Angelina," she said, pointing to herself.

"Adam and Tory," Adam said, indicating himself and then Tory.

The baby cried harder and Angelina's look hardened into impatience. Tory followed her into a dimly lighted room where the baby lay on a bare mattress, undiapered. Angelina noticed that the baby had dirtied himself and grabbed a rag from a pile in the corner. She smeared it across the baby's bottom and threw it back in the corner. Tory cringed as she noticed the angry red rash on the baby's abdomen. The little one looked just as emaciated as Jenny. Tory wondered how old this baby really was.

It wasn't until her eyes adjusted to the darkened room that Tory realized someone else sat in the corner beside the pile of rags. It was a little boy, no more than 6 or 7. His eyes were scarred shut and he sat silently, listening, with the air of a wounded wild animal that isn't sure what his captors will do to him next. As the horror of what she saw began to sink in, Tory felt the room spin. Nausea gripped her. She stumbled out of the room, out the front door, and around the corner of the shanty, retching.

Adam followed and stood beside her as she leaned against the house. He placed a comforting hand on her shoulder. "Pretty bad, huh," he said, sympathy in his voice. "One thing is for sure. We can't let Jenny come back to this."

Tory nodded, wiping her eyes and taking a deep breath. "I'll be OK," she said. "It just hit me when I saw that little boy. His own mother did that to him!"

"Yeah, it's terrible." Adam sighed. "I wish there was some way we could teach her a better way to live. Not to try to alter her culture, but to help her see that she doesn't have to hurt her children to survive." He shook his head. Then he took Tory by the shoulders and turned her to face him. "Are you going to be all right? I don't want to leave you but I need to convince Angelina to let us take Jenny to the orphanage."

Tory smiled weakly. "I'm supposed to be the nerves-of-steel medical person in this bunch, aren't I? Yes, I'm fine. Go do your thing. I'll be praying for you."

Adam disappeared into the house and Tory breathed a prayer of wisdom and courage for him. *And while You're at it, Father, I need an extra dose myself. This is more than I bargained for, but I know there is nothing You ask us to do that You won't also give us the strength for. I just need an emergency ration right now!*

CHAPTER EIGHT

The weeks passed and Tory began to wonder what she ever did with all her time before she came to Honduras. Every day at the orphanage was packed with new experiences. She'd been shocked the first time she saw the block dormitory building that would house the orphans and the caretakers. But as the men poured cement flooring, installed the tile roof, and put plumbing in the bathrooms, the building began to look less like a bomb shelter and more like a comfortable place to live.

She accompanied Dr. Menandez on several trips into the mountains, vaccinating children and assisting with treatments. Although the hospital environment was very different from anything she'd seen in the U.S., she quickly adjusted to it and gained a lot of respect for the dedicated, overworked staff.

Adam and Antonio grilled her daily on her Spanish and she was pleased at her progress. Antonio's darkly handsome looks contrasted sharply with Adam's fair skin and blue eyes, but the two were very much alike in personality. Tory learned that Antonio, a Limpira Indian, was the relative of a king of his people. Orphaned as a child, he was raised by a kind but stern merchant in the town. He'd been compelled to work hard as a young boy and the habits he formed followed him into adulthood. He was the best worker at the orphanage. Tory could see why Anna Giles, the director of Outreach International, had appointed Antonio as the orphanage director. Daily he proved himself worthy.

Tory grabbed every opportunity she could to ride Tamarindo, too. Although she loved the trips to the river with Adam, she took Mr. Allen's warning about the strange man seriously and never rode Tamarindo to the river alone. If Adam was too busy, she contented herself with teaching the spirited gelding how to jump and do figure eights. She even erected a pole bending course and set up barrels for racing.

Early one morning Mr. Allen asked Tory and Adam to go into town to pick up the first orphan to move into the dormitory. "He's a wiry little guy. Name's Nelson," Mr. Allen told them. "He's pretty scarred up from a lot of abuse. He doesn't know his age or remember anything about his parents."

"He *does* know that his parents died when he was little," Adam told Tory as they drove the little silver pickup into Santa Barbara. "Antonio was the one who talked to him about coming to the orphanage, and he gave me a little more information about him. His father's brother took him in after his parents' death, but all he could remember about his uncle's family was horrific abuse. He was burned with live coals anytime somebody thought he did something wrong. He finally ran away to get out of the nightmare."

Tory shuddered. "He probably didn't have much choice if he wanted to live. Things couldn't be much worse than that."

Adam shook his head. "I don't think life on the street offered much improvement," he said soberly. "So when a lady named Doña Theresa in Santa Barbara offered Nelson a place to stay until the orphanage was ready to move into, he jumped at the chance. He's been with Doña Theresa for a few months now. Antonio told me he's real attached to her. This may be hard on both of them."

Before picking up Nelson, Adam stopped in at the hospital so they could check on Jenny. Her improvement was dramatic. Instead of a listless, vacant stare, Jenny watched the nurses come and go with bright, interested eyes.

"Angelina used to visit regularly," one of the nurses told Adam in Spanish, "but the staff never allowed her to feed Jenny. We knew she'd eat her food like she did before. She seemed upset that she'd lost her free meals. She came less often when she realized we weren't going to slack off while she was in the room."

Tory sighed as Adam shared what the nurse told him, bewildered at the total absence of motherly compassion in the woman. She sat on Jenny's bed, cuddling her in her lap. Jenny's abdomen still protruded like a watermelon from malnutrition, but her stick thin arms seemed to be filling out. Tory played pat-a-cake with Jenny, noticing how tiny the child's hands were in comparison to her own.

The young nurse that Tory liked the best hurried into the room holding a bottle of formula. She smiled and handed the bottle to Tory. Then she turned to Adam. Tory caught several of the Spanish words and realized that the nurse was telling them that it was all right to move Jenny to the orphanage now.

"Now?" Tory caught her breath. "Can we really take her?" It seemed almost too good to be true. In all the weeks of visiting, Tory felt herself growing more and more fond of the spunky little girl. She couldn't wait to get her back to the orphanage and shower her with attention, affection, and good food.

Adam, grinning broadly, gathered up Jenny's formula and diapers and the few personal belongings Angelina had left in the room. Tory carried Jenny and they marched down the crowded hallway and out the front door of the hospital to the truck.

"Oh, no," Tory exclaimed. "We don't have a car seat for her. It isn't safe."

Adam laughed and opened the truck door. "It wouldn't do much good to have a car seat," he said. "Notice there are no seat belts, either."

Tory shook her head. "Drive *carefully,* then, OK?"

"Listen to you," Adam said, a teasing tone in his voice. "You've just been a mom for three minutes and you're already a worry wart."

Doña Theresa's home, a cozy rowhouse, snuggled between two others on a steep side street in Santa Barbara. With her round, expressive face and warm hugs, Doña Theresa made Tory feel at home the moment she and Adam walked in her front door carrying Jenny.

"Ooh, what a sweet thing," Doña Theresa cooed, holding her arms out to take Jenny. Jenny drew back and buried her face in Tory's hair. Doña Theresa smiled and patted Tory's arm. "She feels safe with you."

A small boy with a scarred face stood just behind Doña Theresa, gripping a wad of her long skirt and peering at Tory and Adam with questioning brown eyes. Doña Theresa, as if suddenly remembering the reason for their visit, pushed the boy forward.

"And this is my Nelson," she said, tears welling up in her eyes. "He's a special boy, this one. I know he needs to be with you and with the other children, but my house will be far too quiet without him."

Adam knelt down so he could talk to Nelson directly. He began to speak quietly in Spanish, and Nelson listened intently. Adam asked a question, and Nelson nodded. Then he reached out and took Adam's hand.

"He wants to go with us," Adam said as he stood up and shook Doña Theresa's hand. "Thank you for caring for Nelson. We'll come back for visits as often as we can."

Doña Theresa smiled through her tears. She reached out and drew Nelson close to her, enveloping him in a warm bear hug. Tears glistened in Nelson's eyes, too, as they walked out the door to the truck.

Just as they were about to get into the truck, Doña Theresa leaned in close to Adam. "There is something I must tell you," she said solemnly. "I have heard talk in the town. A bad man is saying that he follows you to the river where you swim. He brags that you are weak Americans and he will easily overcome you." Pointing to Adam, she said, "He says he will kill you with his machete and kidnap your woman."

Tory's face flushed scarlet at Doña Theresa's suggestion that she was Adam's "woman," but fear quickly replaced embarrassment as she realized the very real danger they faced. With sweaty palms and a pounding heart, she held Jenny close and slipped into the cab of the truck. She suddenly felt more shaken than when the brakes went out on the mountain in Guatemala.

Adam's face was strained as he helped Nelson into the truck, climbed in beside him, and started the engine. Nelson turned and waved to Doña Theresa until they turned a corner and he could no longer see her.

Suddenly Adam stepped on the brakes and stopped the truck right in the middle of the street. "I think we need to pray right now," he said, a slight quaver to his voice and his knuckles white on the steering wheel. "We didn't come here to live in fear. Our God is plenty big enough to take care of some guy with a machete and we need to ask Him right now for protection. Then I'm going to tell my fear to get lost! Care to join me?" He gave Tory a sideways glance and smiled wanly.

"Yes," Tory said. "I think that's a great idea. I'm with you."

Adam reached around Nelson so he could put his hand on Jenny's arm and on Tory's at the same time.

"Father," he prayed, his voice now strong and sure, "somebody wants to hurt us, but we know that nothing can happen to us without passing by You first. We ask for Your presence with us and for Your protection, now and always. We're here to serve You, and we are asking how to do that. Thanks for our freedom of choice and that we can, through Your Holy Spirit, order the fear out of our lives to make room for Your love. We love You. In Jesus' name we pray, Amen."

They rode in silence the rest of the way back to the orphanage. Once they arrived, the evening passed quickly in a non-stop round of activity. Flor, one of the helpers at the orphanage, had prepared a boys' dorm room for Nelson. Adam and Antonio would take turns staying with him there. As soon as Flor saw Jenny, she hurried to prepare a bed in the girls' room for her.

A pot of red beans seasoned with cilantro bubbled on the coals of Flor's clay oven in the orphanage courtyard. Her *comal* sizzled as she dropped hand-shaped corn tortillas onto its hot surface. Tory's mouth watered. It hadn't taken her long to develop a love for Honduran food. Especially the way Flor prepared it.

That night in her room, Tory pulled out her journal. She stood for a few moments at her window and watched the fireflies dancing on the lawn. They flitted from place to place in utter abandon, leaving streaks of light behind them. *No fear.* She thought of the thousands of droplets of water that cascaded over the rocks in the waterfall at her secret place in Arkansas where she and Kane talked. She thought of Tamarindo's quiet trust in Adam once he realized that Adam was his master, and of Jenny's tiny hand in hers.

No fear. The words seemed to echo in her head as if they'd been spoken from a loudspeaker. She'd seen the words scrawled across T-shirts, but somehow the message didn't seem like the same one. She thought of Adam's words when he prayed this afternoon. *Thank You that we can order the fear out of our lives to make room for Your love.* Somehow she'd always thought of fear as a basic part of her, a shadow that followed her whether she wanted it there or not.

Father, are You trying to tell me that I can let go of fear completely by trusting You completely?

A loud knock at the door jolted Tory's thoughts back to earth. She opened it to see Mr. Allen standing there, his eyes wide.

"I just got a call, Tory. They need you in town at the prison. One of the kids there is hurt. Will you go?"

Tory stared uncomprehending. "Prison? Kids? Why would a child be in prison?"

Mr. Allen shook his head. "No time to explain. Just go. Antonio will take you. He's out in the truck right now waiting."

CHAPTER NINE

Tory blinked in surprise as she followed Antonio to the Santa Barbara prison. A dingy building right on one of the main streets, the prison seemed more like an open barracks than a place where people were locked up for committing crimes.

Just down the street, a huge cathedral towered over the garden that served as the town square. A stone gazebo stood at the center of the garden. People sat on stone benches and watched children spinning tops and begging passersby for money. Scores of tiny shops crowded around the edges of the square where shopkeepers stood in their doorways, calling out the virtues of their products.

"This used to be a governor's mansion," Antonio whispered as they entered the prison courtyard. Everywhere they looked, prisoners lounged in the open area weaving strands of cotton fiber into hammocks.

"It is their livelihood," Antonio explained. "Some of them work in town, but most just work here. The prisoners can check out anytime but must check back in at night."

Around the perimeter of the courtyard Tory could see separate rooms. She peeked into the rooms as they walked by and noticed that each room held 60 to 80 beds, stacked one on top of the other almost to the ceiling. A concrete staircase jutted up to their right. Antonio bounded up these steps with Tory close on his heels.

"The kitchen is up here," Antonio said, glancing over his shoulder to make sure Tory was following him. "Maria is the cook. It's one of her children that is hurt."

Antonio pushed open the heavy wooden door to the kitchen. A huge wood stove sat in the middle of the windowless room billowing smoke into the air. Tory's lungs burned with the acrid smoke and she stifled the urge to run back out the door where she could breathe.

A stack of tortillas sat beside a huge *comal* on top of the stove. Maria had apparently been in the middle of preparing the evening meal when the accident happened. A high-pitched wail pierced the air from a small room just off the kitchen. A curtain hung from a string tacked to the sides of the door frame.

Tory pushed the curtain aside. There on a bare mattress on the floor lay a small boy with an ugly burn covering much of his lower abdomen. His back arched in pain and a look of terror filled his round face. A middle-aged woman bent over the boy, smearing what looked like lard on the burn.

"Un momento," Tory said, kneeling down beside the woman and opening her first-aid bag. She shot Antonio a pleading look. "Explain to Maria, please. The grease will make it worse. Tell her I need to clean the wound and dress it with special medicine."

Antonio spoke quietly but with authority to the woman and she moved back, nodding to Tory. The boy kept his eyes glued to Tory's, and she recognized the same trapped expression that she had seen on the face of the little blind boy in the mountains.

"¿Como se llama?" Tory whispered to the boy. "What is your name?"

"Carlitos," the boy whimpered. His voice had the

raspy quality of a longtime smoker. He let Tory remove his filthy shirt and lay quietly while she fished in her bag for the right supplies. Quite sure that she couldn't trust the prison's water supply, she chose a sterile saltwater solution and gauze sponges to clean the wound. It wasn't until the burn was cleaned and covered with a special dressing that Carlito's eyes left Tory's face.

Tory turned to Antonio. "Please tell Maria that I will come every day to change this dressing, and that she must keep it clean and dry." She smiled at the woman as Antonio delivered her message.

Maria frowned and muttered something Tory could not understand. Just then a strange sound like a kitten mewing came from the corner of the dark room, and Tory looked around, startled. A tiny, malnourished baby lay totally naked on a mat in the corner, his little body nothing more than skin and bones. Next to him sat a little girl, probably about 6 or 7 years old. Her saucy round face and tangled hair framed a pair of beautiful dark eyes. The expression in them seemed almost defiant, as if by sheer force of will she could change her painful circumstances. Another boy, perhaps a little older than the girl, crouched on the other side of the baby.

The boy coughed, his barrel-shaped chest heaving with the effort to breathe. Tory pulled her stethoscope from the first-aid kit and moved closer to the boy. He watched her with wide eyes but did not pull away as she placed the bell of the stethoscope on his chest and listened to his lungs.

"Antonio, ask her what she is feeding the baby. And tell her this boy cannot sleep in this smoky room," Tory demanded, suddenly angry that the mother seemed so careless. He has terrible asthma."

A defeated look crossed Maria's face as Antonio delivered Tory's message. She talked for a long time, explaining something to Antonio. When she finished, Tory raised her eyebrows in a question. Antonio just shook his head. "I'll fill you in on the way home," he said. Tory could hear the frustration in his voice and guessed that he was concerned about the children too.

On the way back to the orphanage, Antonio shared with Tory the story told to him by Carlitos' mother. "Maria is not just a hired cook for the prison," he said, choosing his words carefully as if each one of them hurt as it came out. "She is a prisoner charged with murdering her husband with an ax. He came home drunk, and she says he was going to beat her up. She denies killing him, but the authorities don't believe her. When she came here to prison, her children had nowhere else to go. They live in that little room off the kitchen with her. She says she cannot nurse the baby because her milk is drying up from all the hard work she does preparing food for the prisoners. She has nothing else to give him."

Tears coursed down Tory's cheeks as she listened to Antonio. "We have to do something for the children," she said when he finished. "We can't just stand by and let that baby die of malnutrition."

Antonio nodded. "I agree with you. What do you think we should do?"

"I don't know yet," Tory said grimly. "But I'll think of something."

Early the next morning Tory headed for Tamarindo's pasture, several slices of apple in her pocket for a treat. Both trucks were in use on orphanage business, and Tory knew the only way to get in to see

Carlitos and the other children in the prison today was on horseback.

As soon as she reached the fence, Tamarindo thundered across the pasture for his treat, his neck arched and his mane flying. The early morning sun caught the curve of his muscular hindquarters. Tory realized as she watched the spirited horse run that his coat wasn't just a solid chocolate brown, but a variety of shades from almost black in some spots to a light sandy buff in other places.

Tamarindo nipped playfully at the pieces of apple in Tory's hand. "Ah," she said, laughing and playing along by pulling her hand back just out of reach for a moment. "You're in a mood today, aren't you? That's good, because we have a lot of work to do. There are some children who need us. How about a trip into town?"

"Were you going to invite me?"

Tory turned to see Adam standing behind her munching on one of Doña Chila's fresh tortillas. He held several others in his hand and gave two of them to Tory.

"Breakfast is the most important meal," he said solemnly.

She giggled as she accepted the steaming tortillas. "Thanks," she said. "And yes, I was hoping you could go with me. There's a woman in the prison that has four children living there with her. One is badly burned. That's what this is for." She pointed to the first-aid kit on the ground beside the saddle. "The oldest boy has terrible asthma. I'd bet anything the girl is being abused by the prisoners. And the baby is dying of malnutrition."

"Wow." Adam grimaced. "Sounds like we need to head to town. What are we going to do for the baby?"

Tory shrugged. "I haven't figured that out yet. I'm

77

still thinking."

"Hey, I have an idea." Adam's face brightened as he spoke. "There are some cans of Pediasure formula in that stuff on the shelves in my room. Let's borrow Jenny's old bottle. She doesn't really need it anymore. She ate a whole bowl of oatmeal this morning, almost in one gulp. I'll saddle this guy if you want to collect supplies."

Tory nodded and hurried into the house to gather whatever food she could find that she thought might help the children gain strength. Linda gave her some peanut butter and crackers and packets of dried fruit. She found the Pediasure on the shelf in Adam's room just as he said. She distributed the formula and food items between two heavy burlap bags, then tied the tops of the bags together to form a balanced set of saddlebags.

She waited until Adam mounted Tamarindo, then handed him the bags.

"I'll balance them behind me once I'm up," she stated with a little more assurance than she felt. She hoped Tamarindo wouldn't spook as the bags hung down and smacked his flanks with each step. Cautiously, she swung up into the saddle behind Adam and arranged the bags behind her.

Tamarindo snorted and sidestepped at first when he felt the burlap bags bumping against his sides. Adam leaned close to his ear and talked to him in a calm, reassuring voice and soon he settled in to a steady determined pace. His ears flicked back to listen to Adam, then forward as if anticipating the trip to town.

The prisoners stopped their hammock making as Tory and Adam entered the prison courtyard carrying the supplies. They seemed surprised to see American visitors two days in a row, especially a woman. Tory made a beeline for the stairs that led up to the kitchen, ignoring the curious stares of the prisoners.

Maria stood beside the huge *comal* in the center of the smoky kitchen, patting *masa* dough into tortillas. She smiled shyly when she saw Tory and lowered her eyes as Adam entered the room. Adam greeted her in Spanish and introduced himself, then followed Tory to the little room at the rear of the kitchen. Tory pulled back the grimy curtain. Only the baby lay on the mat in the corner of the smaller room.

"Where is Carlitos?" Tory asked Maria, using her limited Spanish. Maria grunted and nodded toward the courtyard. Tory knelt down beside the baby and opened one of the bags. She pulled out some travel wet wipes that she had saved from her own supplies, a clean cloth diaper, and a tiny T-shirt. Cleaning the baby the best she could, she dressed him and wrapped him in a soft cotton blanket. Adam opened one of the cans of Pediasure and filled Jenny's bottle.

The listless baby turned his face away as Tory touched the nipple of the bottle to his cheek. He seemed to have given up on life. Hot tears sprung to Tory's eyes. How could she help the tiny one *want* to survive? Without really thinking about what she was doing, she began to rock the baby gently back and forth, humming softly. She held the bottle close to his little mouth and dripped a few drops of formula between his lips. As he opened his mouth slightly, Tory saw a number of teeth.

"This is *not* a newborn," she whispered to Adam. "He's at least a year old!"

Tory kept up a steady drip of formula into the baby's mouth and breathed a sigh of relief as he began to swallow. Before long, he turned toward the bottle and actually sucked on the nipple, pulling the life-giving formula into his mouth. She glanced up at Adam and saw tears glistening in his eyes.

"Maybe he'll make it," Adam murmured, wiping his eyes.

The other children filed into the kitchen while Tory fed the baby. They crowded around her, watching their little brother eat. Adam pulled the jar of peanut butter and a box of crackers out of the knapsack. He slathered peanut butter on crackers with a plastic knife and handed them out to the children, talking to them in Spanish all the while.

"This oldest boy with the huffing, puffing breathing is Oscar," Adam told Tory as the children ate their crackers. "He told me he saw our horse tied outside and he wants to ride him. The girl is Dilma. You know Carlitos. And the little one you're holding is Douglas. Dilma told me." He grinned triumphantly. "See what a good medical assistant I am?"

Tory laughed. "Yes. You get an A for admirable assessment skills."

Carlitos burn looked uglier than ever as Tory pulled the old dressing off and cleaned the wound. The boy stood quietly, never flinching even though Tory knew the process had to be painful. The clean dressing in place, she reached into her pocket and pulled out a smiley face sticker and stuck it right to the center of the bandage. Carlitos looked up at her and smiled for the first time since she had first seen him. His teeth were black and rotted away almost to the gumline, but his dark eyes gleamed with pleasure as he poked a stubby finger at the bright yellow sticker.

Before they left, Tory gave Maria several cans of the infant formula and Adam helped her explain the feeding schedule. Maria nodded as if in agreement with the plan, but Tory detected a glint of fear in the woman's eyes and wondered how well she would follow through.

Why would Maria be afraid of something good, Father? Tory mused as she rode behind Adam back to the orphanage. *We're only trying to teach her how to take better care of her children.*

CHAPTER TEN

Even though it was late fall, the days grew hot and muggy. Tiny black mosquitos swarmed around Tory's arms and legs as she waded through the tall grass behind the house to take Tamarindo his treats. She noticed that the gelding swished his tail constantly, fighting the pesky insects, too. She sighed as she looked down at the tiny red spots that peppered her arms and legs.

"It's the price of living in paradise, I guess," she muttered, brushing mosquitos from Tamarindo's face. She slipped the bridle in place and let the reins fall to the ground while she headed for the shed to get the saddle. As her eyes adjusted to the light, she saw a small folded up piece of paper stuck in the small opening just behind the saddle horn. She pulled it out and opened it.

The funny little stick drawing on the paper showed three figures, one with a full beard, one shorter figure with long hair, and one taller one with short hair. The words under the drawing said, "You have two devoted friends, God and me. Adam."

Tory laughed out loud and read the little note over several times before she stuck it in her pocket. As she dragged the saddle from its place and hoisted it on her hip to carry it out to the pasture, she thought of the first few days she'd known Adam and how worried she had been that he wouldn't want to be friends. She smiled at the memory.

"He's like a brother only better," she told Tamarindo as she brushed him down before saddling him. "I don't want anything to change that."

She picked a bright-blue flower from a clump of grass beside one of the fenceposts and tucked it into her shirt pocket, then swung into the saddle and cantered the gelding across the field to the gate and up the lane to the orphanage. Nelson and Antonio squatted side by side in the garden spot inspecting the corn shoots that were just breaking through the ground. As soon as Nelson saw Tory and Tamarindo coming, he jumped up and ran toward them.

"El caballo," he shouted, waving his arms.

Just then Adam appeared around the corner of the building pushing a wheelbarrow filled with broken pieces of cement he had cracked out of the orphanage courtyard to dump in the septic system drainage ditch. "*Si,* Nelson," he said "that is a horse."

"Do you want to ride today, Nelson?" Tory asked, reaching down for the boy's hand. Nelson shot Antonio a questioning look. Antonio nodded and spoke something in Spanish to the boy. Nelson grinned from ear to ear and grabbed Tory's hand, allowing her to pull him up behind her on Tamarindo's back.

Reining the gelding in a circle, Tory guided him close to the place where Adam stood watching them. She pulled the blue flower from her pocket, leaned over, and tucked it into his hair just behind his right ear. "Thanks for the note," she whispered. "I loved it."

Adam grinned. "It's true, you know."

Tory nodded. "I know."

She reined Tamarindo toward the highway and nudged him into a canter. Nelson clung to her like an organ-grinder's monkey, shrieking with delight.

Crossing the highway, Tory found the old cow path that led to the old bridge and the waterfall. The smooth path, pounded free of rocks and sticks by thousands of hooves over the decades, made an excellent bridle trail.

As they rode along, Tory thought back over the past eight weeks. Every day without fail, even on the weekends, she and Adam had made the trip into town to visit Douglas, Carlitos, Dilma, and Oscar in the prison. The children loved the peanut butter and crackers and other treats they brought. Every day they all took a walk in the fresh air and sunshine after Douglas got his bottle, his bath, and a fresh change of clothing.

Carlitos' burn gradually healed and the dressing was no longer necessary. He liked the extra attention, though, and Tory fiddled with applying the medicine sometimes much longer than was really necessary. She couldn't resist Carlitos' dancing dark eyes and mischievous smile. All of the children but Oscar were thriving on the daily visits. His lungs continued to get worse with every day he spent in the smoke-filled kitchen with Maria.

"I have to get those kids out of that prison," Tory said, not sure who she was talking to, since neither Nelson nor Tamarindo could understand her. Tamarindo flicked an ear back in her direction. Tory patted his neck. "You tell me, Tamarindo. How can we convince Maria to let them come to the orphanage? Even if it's just during the week, it will give them a chance to get healthier."

They rounded a curve in the trail and suddenly up ahead Tory saw the dark figure of a man step into the trail, a machete gleaming in his hand. She stifled a scream and jerked the reins back. Tamarindo stopped so fast he almost sat down on his haunches. Nelson gripped

Tory's waist so tightly she almost couldn't breathe.

In one swift movement, Tory wheeled Tamarindo around in the trail and dug her heels into his sides. She leaned low over his neck as he sprang into a dead run, his mane whipping her face like stinging nettles. Nelson whimpered, but never released his iron grip on Tory's waist.

As they thundered into the yard, Adam and Antonio dropped what they were doing and rushed to meet them. "What happened?" Adam asked as he grabbed Tamarindo's reins.

"It was that man," Tory blurted out when she could speak again. "He stepped into the path in front of us. He had a machete." She helped Nelson down and dismounted herself, her legs trembling so violently she could hardly stand up.

Antonio put an arm around Nelson's shoulder and began asking him questions in Spanish, giving him a chance to talk about the wild ride. Nelson's eyes were wide with fear as he told Antonio about the man in the trail.

A grim expression on his face, Adam walked Tamarindo around in large circles on the patch of lawn beside the garden to cool him down. Flor came out of the orphanage kitchen, little Jenny on her hip. Jenny gurgled with delight when she saw Tory. Flor put her down on the grass and she crawled toward Tory, her huge abdomen dragging the ground as she moved.

Tory momentarily forgot her fright in the joy of seeing Jenny move about so freely. In the few short months since she'd come to the orphanage, Jenny's weight had doubled and she had blossomed from a listless, helpless baby into an active, energetic child. Her belly stayed large, but Dr. Menandez assured them that with time, it too would return to the size of a normal child's stomach.

Sinking down into the grass, Tory pulled Jenny up into her lap and nuzzled the fuzz of shiny dark hair that was beginning to grow on Jenny's head. Jenny laughed and curled her tiny arms around Tory's neck.

"You're good medicine, young lady," Tory whispered to the little girl.

Adam led Tamarindo around to the spot where Tory and Jenny sat. "We'd better head into town before it gets too late," he said, his voice sounding calmer. "They'll be waiting for us at the prison. I have the bags of goodies all ready to go." He pointed to the gunny sacks leaning against the wall of the orphanage.

Tory nodded and handed Jenny back to Flor. She grabbed the bags and swung them up onto the saddle, then climbed up herself. Antonio waved goodbye from the garden where he'd put Nelson to work setting out tomato plants. "Be careful," he called.

It was late afternoon by the time Tory and Adam arrived at the prison. Groups of people huddled on the sidewalk outside the prison, speaking in hushed tones. Adam tied Tamarindo to a tree and followed Tory down the steps into the courtyard. None of the prisoners were working on hammocks. Instead, they all stood solemnly in a circle in the middle of the work area, staring at something on the ground. Maria sat in the middle of the circle beside the object. Her eyes were shut tight and she rocked back and forth as if trying to console herself.

Tory's heart jumped to her throat as she saw the tiny form, covered with a ragged blanket. She rushed over to the circle of men and pushed her way to the place where Maria sat.

"Maria, what happened," she cried, grabbing the woman's shoulder and shaking her gently. Maria slowly opened her eyes, reached out, and pulled the blanket back. It was baby Douglas. His tiny face looked strangely peaceful except for a mark on his forehead. It was hard to believe he was really dead.

Hot tears streamed down Tory's cheeks. She bent down and touched the baby's face, remembering it lit up with happy smiles as she carried him around the streets of the town on their daily visits. A dull ache crept into her chest and settled around her heart. She looked up to see Adam gazing down at Douglas, tears filling his blue eyes and spilling down onto the front of his shirt.

Adam began to question the inmates that stood around the circle, trying to find out what happened. Maria just shook her head and wailed softly when he talked to her. But gradually, he pieced the story together. "One of the guards had been carrying Douglas around, apparently drunk," he told Tory, his voice choked with emotion. "Douglas slipped out of his arms and fell on the concrete. His fragile little body couldn't stand the trauma and he died instantly."

Tory felt a tug at her sleeve and looked down to see Carlitos and Dilma, their eyes wide with fear, standing beside her. She slipped her arms around them and hugged them close. "Oh, how I wish I could talk to you," she sobbed into their hair. "I would try to think of something comforting to tell you, although right now I can't imagine what that would be."

CHAPTER ELEVEN

The next day passed in a blur of pain for Tory. She barely remembered the trip back to the orphanage on Tamarindo. She watched silently as Adam gathered several boards and fashioned a tiny casket for Douglas, lining it with a swatch of blue satin he cut from a woman's dress he found in the clothing supply. He avoided looking at anyone most of the time as he worked, but once when she caught his eye, she saw the deep pain that she felt in her own heart mirrored there.

When the little casket was finished, Adam placed it gently in Tory's arms. "Let's go," he said, his voice choked with emotion. "Douglas deserves a funeral."

It appeared that no one had touched the baby's body since the day before. The prisoners gathered around in a sober huddle as Tory and Adam placed the casket on the courtyard floor beside Douglas and reverently lifted his body into it. Together, they carried the casket to the little village church in the center of the square. Maria and the other children followed close behind. Several prisoners accompanied them.

The priest met the little company at the front door of the church and escorted them in. Tory and Adam followed him down the aisle to an altar in the very front of the room. They placed the casket on a table in front of the altar and stepped back. Tory stood beside Maria, slipping an arm around her waist and holding her close as tears slipped down both their faces.

Dilma took her place between Maria and Tory. Tory glanced over at Adam to see Oscar and Carlitos each holding one of his hands. The boys' glances shifted back and forth nervously, taking in all the strange sights in the church. Adam knelt down and whispered something to Carlitos. He pointed up to a statue of Jesus that stood in the front of the church. Carlitos nodded and appeared calmer.

The priest began to speak, his words lilting and musical, like a chant in an ancient cathedral. Tory could pick out a word here and there. It sounded as if he were describing heaven.

That's good, Father, Tory prayed silently. *Maria needs the comforting words of her pastor right now more than ever.*

Suddenly Tory felt Maria's body slump against her arm. She glanced at the woman's face, an ashen gray against her dark dress, and realized she was about to faint. Before Tory could decide what to do Maria sank to the floor, unconscious. The priest took one look at the unresponsive woman, closed his prayer book, and walked away. One by one the prisoners shuffled back to the prison. Only Tory and Adam remained with Maria and her children.

"I'd like to strangle that man," Adam whispered fiercely as he bent over Maria's still form on the cobblestone floor.

Tory sat down and pulled Maria's head into her lap. "Why?" she asked, mystified by his angry reaction to someone he just met.

Adam shook his head. "Did you catch any of what he was saying just before Maria fainted? He was telling her that Douglas is in limbo and will stay there until she can raise the money to get him out."

Tory stared at Adam in utter disbelief. "He *what?*"

"You heard me right." Adam's eyes flashed with anger. "No wonder Maria passed out. She may not have the best mothering techniques in the world, but she loves her children the best way she knows how."

Smoothing Maria's hair back from her damp forehead, Tory studied the woman's face thoughtfully. "But how can he tell her such things? That's not what the Bible teaches. It says death is like a sleep until Jesus comes. It will seem like only an instant to the one who dies. Douglas will wake up to see Jesus' face at the Second Coming. No one goes to limbo *or* to hell when they die. The only people that will burn will be the ones God has to destroy with fire after the judgment is all over and it's clear they've chosen Satan's way instead of God's. That priest must know that if he's studied his Bible."

Adam sighed. "I agree with you and I can't answer for the priest. I only know what I heard him say." He stood up and looked around the church. "Right now we have to figure out how to get Maria back to the prison and what to do with Douglas's little body."

Just then Maria's eyes fluttered open and she tried to sit up. Tory steadied her until she regained her balance. Adam spoke a few words to Maria in Spanish and she closed her eyes again, tears squeezing out from under her eyelids and trickling down her cheeks.

When she tried again to get up, Tory supported her back and helped her stand. Then she walked slowly along beside her while Adam carried the casket. Dilma clung to her mother's skirt, and Oscar and Carlitos walked stiffly beside Adam, their expressions pinched and sad.

Once back at the prison, the officials gave Adam

permission to bury Douglas at the orphanage. Adam discussed a burial site with Maria and together they decided on a spot behind the orphanage under a guanabanas tree. Maria had never been to the orphanage, but Adam described the grounds to her and she seemed happy with the place he suggested.

Tory stood close beside Maria as Adam carried the tiny casket out to the truck. She could feel Maria trembling.

"Adam," she called after him. "Go on without me. I'm going to stay with Maria for awhile."

Adam nodded and disappeared out the door. Tory helped Maria up the steep concrete steps to the kitchen. The prisoners were already starting to gather for their evening meal, and Tory knew Maria was in no shape to prepare it.

Father, she prayed, her mind racing, *I have to be able to communicate with Maria so she can tell me what to do to prepare this meal. Please give me the gift of languages like You gave the apostles at Pentecost so long ago so I can speak to her and understand what she is saying to me.*

A sense of calm settled over her as she stoked the fire in the cement oven under the *comal.* When she opened her mouth to speak to Maria, the words came out in perfect Spanish. And she understood every word Maria said to her in answer to her questions.

Maria rested on a mat in the corner of the kitchen and directed Tory to the bag of *masa* for mixing with warm water to make the tortillas. Patting out the flat corn cakes felt awkward at first but soon Tory was flipping perfect round tortillas onto the *komal* to grill. Dilma and Oscar helped her scoop the finished tortillas into the serving buckets. Carlitos sat on the mat beside Maria, his eyes wide, watching the unusual proceedings.

At one point, Maria slipped from her mat and reached behind the curtain that separated the little sleeping room from the rest of the kitchen. When she returned, she carried a worn leather Bible in her hands. As soon as Tory finished cooking the tortillas for the prisoners supper and prepared enough for Maria and the children to eat, too, Maria held the Bible out to Tory.

"Show me," she said pleadingly in Spanish. "Show me what this book says about where my Douglas is right now."

Tory took the Bible and sat still for a long time, holding the book in her lap. *Send Your Spirit to teach me what to say to Maria,* she prayed silently. *I need Your words and I need wisdom to speak them for You. Thank You for hearing me and answering in a way that will bring understanding to Maria's mind about Your love and grace. In Jesus' name, Amen.*

As she flipped the pages of the Bible, Tory felt a surge of panic. The Spanish words seemed to run together like hieroglyphic characters. She took a deep breath as she tried to find Ecclesiastes and found that if she concentrated on each one, she *could* read the words. She turned to chapter nine and ran her finger down the column to verse five.

"Maria, it says here that 'The living know that they shall die, but the dead know not anything.'"

She turned to the second chapter of Acts and found verse 29. "'And here is a verse in which Peter is talking about King David. He says that David is 'dead and buried.' And here in 1 Corinthians 15, verses 20 through 23, it says 'now is Christ risen from the dead and become firstfruits of them that slept . . . for as in Adam all die, even so in Christ shall all be made alive. But every man in his own order: Christ the firstfruits;

afterward they that are Christ's at his coming' (KJV). Verses 51 and 52 say 'We shall not all sleep, but we shall all be changed, in a moment, in the twinkling of an eye, at the last trump: for the trumpet shall sound, and the dead shall be raised incorruptible, and we shall be changed' (KJV).

"And 1 Thessalonians 4:16 and 17 says, 'The Lord himself shall descend from heaven with a shout, with the voice of the archangel, and with the trump of God; and the dead in Christ shall rise first: then we which are alive and remain shall be caught up together with them in the clouds to meet the Lord in the air: and so shall we ever be with the Lord'" (KJV).

Tory looked up from her reading and saw tears spilling down Maria's cheeks. She closed the Bible and set it aside. "Maria, is the reading hurting you more?" she asked, moving to Maria's side and slipping her arm around her shoulder.

"No," Maria said. "I want to hear it. I don't understand what it means, but I don't hear anything about my Douglas being in limbo."

Tory hugged her close. "And you won't find it anywhere in the Bible," she said. "Douglas is resting until Jesus comes again to take us all to a place where no one will ever die again. And you will have Douglas back in your arms."

Maria's face beamed through her tears. "It's good," she said. "I want to know more about the Bible. Will you teach me?"

Tory nodded as she picked up the Bible and handed it back to Maria. She looked up to see Adam standing in the doorway. "Another day," she said. "Soon."

"Are you ready to go, Tory?" Adam asked, squatting down to hug Carlitos and Oscar as they ran to him.

Maria stood up and pushed Dilma gently forward, too. "I want you to take the children," she said in Spanish. "Teach them so they can read like you. It's bad here. They should go with you."

Adam searched the children's faces. "Are you ready to come with us, Oscar? Dilma? Carlitos?" Each of them solemnly nodded. Adam looked up at Tory and grinned. "Well, Ma, I guess your family just grew."

The children crowded into the cab with Tory and Adam, Carlitos on Dilma's lap in the middle and Oscar on Tory's lap next to the door. As they began the drive back to the orphanage, Adam turned to Tory, a look of wonder on his face.

"Did I hear what I thought I heard back there? It sounded like you were speaking and understanding Spanish like a pro."

Tory laughed softly. "I guess I was, wasn't I?" She shook her head. "Only it wasn't me doing it. God did it so I could help Maria. It was a miracle."

Dilma snuggled up close to Tory's side and closed her eyes. Carlitos was already asleep on her lap. Tory nodded her head toward the children. "And here is another miracle. These kids are going to have the chance little Douglas never had."

Adam nodded, a sad look on his face. Tory could tell he missed Douglas as much as she did. He glanced over at her and smiled.

"We have been through a lot together, haven't we?" he said. "You're probably the best friend I've ever had. I don't want to ever do anything to mess that up." He paused and stared straight ahead. Tory held her breath, wondering what he would say next.

"Everyone I know who had a good friend and then tried to make it more," he continued, "you know, like boyfriend and girlfriend, ended up breaking up and not having their friendship anymore. I don't want to let that happen to us."

Tory gulped, feeling her cheeks flaming hot in her embarrassment at the turn the conversation was taking. Thankful for the darkness in the cab, she blurted, "I don't either. I want things to stay just like they are."

"Good," Adam said quickly, glancing over at Tory with a look of relief on his face. "I'm glad we talked."

They rode in silence for a few minutes. By this time Oscar, too, had nodded off, leaning his head against the truck window. A full moon rose over the mountains directly in front of them. The thin blue moonlight flooded the cab with an almost silver glow. Tory thought of the little grave on the hillside behind the orphanage and of the day when the sky would open wide and Jesus would appear, brighter than the sun and the moon together.

"Are you thinking about Douglas?" Adam asked softly.

Tory smiled. "Yes," she said. "I was thinking that when Jesus comes I want to be somewhere close to his little grave. I want to see Maria's face when she sees how perfect he is in his resurrection body and gets to hold him again."

"Yep," Adam said. "And then, when she's done hugging him, it'll be *my* turn."

CHAPTER TWELVE

Fall eased into winter and day-to-day activities at the orphanage developed a rhythm that Tory found relaxing and comforting. No one seemed in a big hurry to go anywhere or do anything, but everything that needed to get done eventually got accomplished. She learned to respect siesta time when everyone in the town shut down their shops and businesses and took a nap. The children, too, never questioned the custom of resting everyday after lunch.

Dilma, Oscar, and Carlitos thrived on life away from the prison. Tory and Adam made sure they made at least weekly visits to Maria, but the children were always eager to return to the orphanage at the end of each visit. Oscar's asthma cleared up completely during his first week at the orphanage and only recurred if he spent more than a few minutes in the smoky prison kitchen.

Every week, Maria asked something about the Bible and Tory studied with her, looking up verse after verse to answer her questions. Maria seemed hungry to know as much as she could about Jesus' coming, heaven, the judgment day, and what happens to a person when they die. She asked about the strange animals in the book of Daniel and the huge statue made of different kinds of metal that was knocked down by a rock that became a huge mountain. Tory was amazed as she studied with Maria that the Spanish terms came easily and she was able to explain the difficult concepts without stumbling over the words.

To Tory's delight, in late November Jenny began to walk. At first she pulled herself up along one of the block walls of the courtyard and inched along, steadying herself against the wall. Then one morning she let go of the wall and tottered, unsupported, across the courtyard. Dilma saw her first and shrieked, "Look, Tory, Jenny's walking!"

All the children ran to Jenny, hugging her and patting her on the back. Carlitos planted a kiss on her cheek and chortled with delight. Jenny sat down, beaming with pride at her latest accomplishment. Tory ran to the little girl and scooped her up in her arms.

"Jenny, you are fantastic," she whispered in her ear. "I am *so* proud of you." She thought of the frail, listless child she'd first met in the hospital. It was hard to believe this was the same girl. She wondered how long it would be before Jenny would try to speak. She made sounds to let others know of her needs, but as far as Tory knew, no one had ever heard her try to say a word.

Antonio and Flor looked up from the screen in the center of the courtyard where they were threshing the winter's supply of rice and smiled proudly. Tory knew how important the rice supply was to their survival and knew it would take more than a baby's first steps to convince them to stop the process. She and Adam had helped with the actual rice harvest. It was a backbreaking job done with a hand-held sickle. It took Tory awhile to catch on to the rhythm of cutting: pull a handful of rice stalks taut, chop it with the sickle just below the rice heads, pull, chop, pull, chop . . .

The rice stalks cut, they placed them on a screen door suspended a foot or so above the ground on cement blocks with a tarp underneath to catch the grains of rice as they fell. Then Antonio or Flor pounded the stocks with sticks to loosen the grains.

The outside covering of the rice, called chaff, stayed on top of the screen and the heavier grains of rice fell through to the tarp below.

Tory put Jenny down and hurried over to help Antonio and Flor scoop the rice into burlap bags for storage. She liked the rice harvest, as grueling as it was, almost as much as the corn harvest. To harvest the corn, they waited until the ears of corn dried on the stalk in early November. Then everyone pitched in to walk up and down the corn rows, breaking off the dried ears and dropping them in a gunnysack each one carried. With the dried corn collected, they all sat in a circle on the cement in the courtyard and pulled the dry outer leaves, or shucks, off the ears.

Tory glanced over at the corncrib behind the orphanage. It was the size of a small garage and it was filled to the top with dried corncobs, just waiting to be ground into *masa* for tortillas. She looked down at her hands, still cracked and dry from the tedious harvesting and husking process, but she felt a sense of accomplishment unlike any she'd ever felt before. She knew the work she'd done in the cornfield meant the difference between eating and going hungry for the children in the orphanage.

Just as they were filling the last burlap bag with rice, Tory heard the pound of hooves coming up the lane. She looked up to see Adam crouching low over Tamarindo's neck and urging the horse into a dead run. She ran out of the courtyard and partway down the lane to meet him.

"What's wrong?" she shouted as the horse and rider

drew closer. Adam pulled Tamarindo to a stop just in front of Tory and slipped from his back as easily as any rodeo bareback rider. He gave her a strange look.

"Nothing. Why?"

Tory shook her head and turned away. "You two. I thought you had some kind of bad news the way you were running. I never thought you'd be running just to be *running.*"

Nelson appeared behind Tory and pulled on her shirttail. "I want to ride like that," he said in Spanish. "Teach me to ride, please."

Adam gave Tory a triumphant look. "See? Someone appreciates the fine art of horsemanship." He led Tamarindo in a wide circle in front of the orphanage to cool him down. After walking several large circles the gelding's breathing evened out and Adam led him back to the spot where Nelson stood watching.

"OK, young man," he said in Spanish, squatting down to look Nelson in the eye. "I'll teach you to ride, but you have to be willing to start at the beginning. Are you?"

Nelson nodded eagerly.

"The first thing you need to know when you're learning to ride is how to approach a horse without getting kicked. Very important. Right Tory?" Adam winked at her and she smiled back at him, remembering Blackberry and her flying hooves.

Adam handed Tory the reins. "I'll demonstrate the right way to approach a horse whether he's in the field or in a stall." He made a wide circle and walked up to Tamarindo from the front. "It's very important not to come up to a horse from the back where he can't see you. Horse's eyes don't work the same way ours do. They can see a wider range, but their eyes don't focus the same. They focus on one object and the rest of their field of vision is blurry. If they see movement and hear something behind them but can't tell what it is, their instinct is to kick out at it before it attacks them."

Nelson nodded, a serious look of concentration on his face. Tory could see that he was serious about learning to ride. Adam spoke softly as he drew closer to the horse.

"It's important to let the horse hear your voice as you approach him. He can tell by your voice tone that you're calm and that will reassure him. Don't wave your arms around or make any sudden movements. He can't follow those rapid moves fast enough to feel safe and it's likely he'll spook and do something neither one of you will like."

Adam took the reins back from Tory and walked Tamarindo over to the spot where Nelson stood. Tamarindo seemed to sense his role as a teacher and cooperated beautifully. Adam held the reins out to Nelson.

"Go ahead and lead him, Nelson," he said. "Hold the reins or lead rope in your right hand and walk a little to the horse's left and just ahead of him. Hang on to the reins or lead rope just below the bit or just under the halter if he's wearing one. Give him a gentle tug as you move forward and make sure he is a step behind you. If he walks too fast and starts crowding you, stop. Make him come to a complete stop and start over again."

Nelson took the reins and started walking with Tamarindo just behind him, docile as a lamb. Nelson looked back over his shoulder and grinned happily at Tory and Adam. He led the gelding in a large circle, then back to where he started.

"Great job!" Adam squeezed Nelson's shoulder and smiled proudly at him. "That's probably enough lesson for today. Want to ride behind me and go for a *real* ride?"

Nelson's eyes brightened and he nodded eagerly.

Adam flipped the reins up over Tamarindo's neck and vaulted smoothly into the saddle. Tory boosted Nelson up behind him in the saddle and stepped back. She had a feeling this would be no quiet little trail ride.

Tamarindo trembled in anticipation as Adam hunkered down in the saddle. "Hang on tight to my waist, Nelson," he said as he loosened the reins slightly and squeezed his legs into Tamarindo's sides. The horse leaped into a canter without a moment's hesitation. He seemed to sense that his riders wanted adventure and he was ready for it, too. His canter flattened into a dead run before he'd gone a hundred yards. The trio soon disappeared down the trail to the river.

Tory felt a tug at the hem of her shorts and looked down to see Jenny grinning up at her, fuzzy dark hair framing her round face. She bent down and picked up the little girl.

"El caballo," Jenny said, pointing in the direction Tamarindo had disappeared. *"Rapido."* Tory stared at Jenny in disbelief, then laughed with delight, hugging her close.

"Yes, Jenny, the horse *is* fast. You're *talking!"*

Antonio and Flor dropped their rice bags and ran to Tory's side, along with the rest of the children. Oscar and Dilma patted Jenny's back, congratulating her in excited tones. Jenny, suddenly shy, buried her face in Tory's hair and wouldn't look at anyone.

The Ford pickup rumbled up the lane and stopped beside the huddled group. Mr. Allen jumped out, a puzzled expression on his face. "Is everything all right?" he asked. "I thought I heard screaming and thundering hooves like that horse had been shot out of a cannon."

Tory laughed. "Everything's fine. Adam just took Nelson for a fast ride, and Jenny spoke her first words.

We were all excited about it, that's all."

Mr. Allen looked relieved. Well, good," he said. "The reason I came up here was to tell you that a group of students from a university in Michigan will be arriving next week to help us build the water tank and finish up construction here. They'll be holding a series of meetings in town, too."

"All right!" Tory knew how badly the orphanage needed the water-storage tank. When the dry season hit, water could become scarce. She dreaded the tedious chore of hauling water from the river for laundry and bathing. Then she thought of the incomplete orphanage rooms and the tight quarters in the main house. "But where will they stay?"

Mr. Allen pointed up the road to the north. "The fish hatchery," he said. "They have a dormitory building there that has a group kitchen. It's not far, maybe a mile or two."

"It's where the groups that come in always stay," Antonio piped up. "It's a good place."

"Tory, I'd like you and Adam to ride up there this morning and check things out. Just make sure everything is ready for the group." Mr. Allen got back into the truck and waved goodbye. "I'm glad everyone is OK."

As Tory watched him drive away, she thought of the responsibility Mr. Allen carried for the safety and well-being of the group. *It's not an easy job he has, Father. So much can happen that none of us can control. I know that's why he's learned to trust You so much. It's the only way to survive.*

CHAPTER THIRTEEN

The week passed quickly, filled with preparations for the arrival of the students from the American university. Tory fell in love with the setting at the fish hatchery immediately. The long dormitory building, with its open kitchen and dining area at one end, sat at the top of a hill surrounded by lush, green gardens. A rock fence, three feet high and two feet wide bordered the yard and marked the crest of the hill where the grounds plunged steeply down to the fish ponds.

As Tory and Adam waited by the front gate for the bus to arrive, Tory climbed up on the wall and peered down into the closest fish pond. Suddenly a long, slender snout shot out of the water, rows of sharp teeth flashing in the sunlight. "Alligator!" she shouted. "There are alligators in these ponds."

Adam hurried over to the wall and climbed up beside her, but by then the reptile had disappeared. "Yeah, right," he teased. "You're seeing things." He slipped his arm around her waist. "But you're still my favorite person."

Tory returned his hug. "You're mine, too." She jumped down from the wall just as the bus pulled up next to the gate. A stream of guys and girls carrying sleeping bags and backpacks piled off the bus, chattering excitedly. A slightly older guy, Tory guessed him to be about 26, came toward Tory and Adam with a friendly smile and an outstretched hand. "Hi, I'm Greg

Miles," he said. "I'm one of the sponsors for this group."

Adam stepped forward and grasped Greg's hand. "I'm Adam Hartman. And this is Tory Butler. She's a nurse working with us at the orphanage."

"Hi, Greg," Tory said, extending her hand. Greg's handshake was warm and firm, and he looked at Tory with a steady, confident gaze. She noticed that his eyes were a light golden brown with flecks of green. His sandy brown hair was tousled from the long bus ride.

"It's a pleasure to meet you, Tory," he said, running his fingers through his hair in a futile attempt to straighten it. He pointed up to the dorm. "Is this where we'll be staying?"

Adam nodded. "Yep. Let us show you the rooms, then we'll help you unload."

Within an hour, all 35 students and sponsors were settled comfortably into their rooms, girls at one end of the building and guys at the other. As soon as Tory had found out that she and Adam were to stay at the fish hatchery with the students, she'd spread out her sleeping bag on a bottom bunk in one of the girls' rooms.

A tall, willowy girl with long, golden-brown hair plunked her backpack on the bottom bunk just opposite Tory's. She smiled at Tory, her clear blue eyes shining. "I'm so glad to finally be here," she said. "I've looked forward to this trip for ever so long. I can't believe you get to stay here all the time. How exciting."

Tory laughed. "Yes. Exciting is a good word for it— sometimes. Then other times it's just hard work and long hours. But it's worth it. By the way, I'm Tory Butler."

"I'm sorry, I should have introduced myself," the girl said. "I'm Jodie Newfelt."

"I'm glad to meet you, Jodie," Tory said. "I'm really glad your group is here. We've been looking forward to the help on the orphanage and building the water-storage tank. It will make a huge difference for the children."

Later, in the kitchen, as Tory and Jodie worked together peeling potatoes for the evening meal, Jodie leaned close to Tory and whispered, "Who is that guy that was with you when we drove up in the bus this afternoon?"

"You mean Adam?" Tory pointed across the dining room to where Adam stood talking with a group of students. "We're working together at the orphanage. He's a great guy. Why?"

Jodie shrugged. "Oh, no reason. I just think he's gorgeous. Are you two, uh, going out or anything?"

"No, we're not," Tory said a little more emphatically than she meant to. "We're just friends. That's all."

"Good," Jodie said with a shy smile. "I'd like to get to know him better, but I didn't want to interfere if he was, you know, *taken*."

Tory felt a tap on her shoulder and turned to see Greg standing behind her, a paring knife in his hand. "I came to save you ladies from potato peeling solitude. May I join you?"

Tossing him a potato, Tory laughed and said, "Sure, have at it."

The food preparation time passed quickly with Greg and Jodie to talk to. As they gave each other quick histories of their lives Tory discovered that Greg planned to be a minister and was majoring in theology. She liked his honesty and his clear, direct communication style. He asked Tory lots of questions about her family and her horses and her goals and dreams in life.

At one point, when Greg excused himself for a few minutes to speak to one of the group members, Jodie whispered in Tory's ear, "I think he likes you. I've never seen him so interested in a girl."

Tory blushed and shrugged her shoulders. "Nah. He's just being nice."

"You just wait and see," Jodie insisted. "Guys don't act like *that* when they're just being nice."

The next morning, Tory sat in the dining room with the university students waiting for the breakfast crew to finish cooking a big pot of hot cereal. She glanced down the table and noticed Jodie sidling up to Adam, asking him a question that she couldn't hear for all the noise in the room. She watched his face as Jodie talked to him, wondering how he would react to the attractive girl. A strange painful feeling welled up in her that she couldn't quite pinpoint.

I should be happy for Adam that a girl as nice as Jodie likes him. What's wrong with me?

Suddenly a huge green dragon-like creature fell from the rafters above the long table and landed, hissing and scratching, on the table surface. Jodie and the other girls jumped back, screaming, as the animal scuttled toward them, its mouth open wide.

The hatchery guard ran into the room and caught the creature, tying its legs with twine so it couldn't get away. Immediately, Adam approached the guard. "What are you going to do with this iguana?" he asked.

The guard smiled and licked his lips. "I will eat it for supper," he said in Spanish.

"No, you can't do that." Adam reached for the animal and to Tory's surprise, the guard gave it up without protest. Adam held the iguana in his lap and slowly stroked its leathery back until it fell asleep.

Jodie sat close beside Adam all through breakfast. She even petted the iguana as long as it kept its eyes closed. As soon as the meal was over, Adam and Greg took the iguana out into the garden area and let it go.

All week the group worked at the orphanage making blocks for the new water tower, finishing the dormitory rooms, and mixing concrete to use as mortar to secure the new clay tiles for the roof. Tory worked with the roof crew, placing the U-shaped tiles in place and "gluing" them with cement. Greg acted as foreman of the roofing crew, so Tory had plenty of chances to talk with him.

When the meetings started at the church, Maria sat on the very front row every single evening. Adam had gotten permission for her to be released from prison on pass to attend. She beamed with pleasure when she saw Tory "on stage" singing with the students during the musical part of the worship service.

Each night Greg and several other theology students in the group presented the Bible studies, with Antonio and Adam acting as interpreters. Maria soaked up every word. Tory noticed that she brought her old leather Bible with her, opening it and trying to find the verses the speakers focused on.

On the third night of the meetings a strange man walked into the church and sat in one of the back pews. Tory glanced at him frequently from her place near the front, for his face looked oddly familiar. All evening she pondered, trying to figure out where she'd seen him before. Every night thereafter, the man came back, listening intently to the presentations. Still, Tory couldn't figure out why his face seemed so embedded in her memory.

With all the activity going on, Tory took care that the children still got the attention and affection they needed. She took breaks during her roofing duties to hold Jenny and to play games with Dilma, Oscar, and Carlitos. Adam brought Tamarindo up from the pasture at least three times a week and continued Nelson's horsemanship lessons.

Tory noticed that Jodie stopped her work to stand close to Adam whenever he brought Tamarindo to the orphanage. She overheard her begging Adam to teach her to ride, too. Adam was friendly and kind to Jodie, but focused on Nelson's progress, never offering to include her in the lessons.

One morning as Adam galloped Tamarindo up the lane to the orphanage, Nelson stood on the bottom rung of the ladder leading up to the roof where Tory was working with Greg.

"Tory," Nelson called. "Come here."

Tory slid on the tiles to the edge of the roof. "What is it, Nelson?" she asked in Spanish.

Nelson hung his head and poked at one of the ladder rungs. "I want you to help with my lesson," he said reluctantly. He turned and pointed at Jodie, already making her way to the lawn area where Adam always taught the horsemanship lessons. "Not her."

"Why? What is wrong with her?" Tory asked, mystified at the boy's insistence.

Nelson raised his eyes to Tory's, and she could see the pain and fear in them. "You are Mama, and Adam, he is Papa," he said. He glared up at Greg on the roof. "Not him."

All at once it dawned on Tory that Nelson had paired her with Adam and felt that his family and all the security it represented to him was being threatened by outside intruders. She scooted down the ladder and knelt down beside Nelson.

"We *all* care about you, Nelson," she said, softly. "Nothing will change that. Even when we go back to the United States, we'll never, ever forget you. Do you understand what I'm saying?"

Nelson nodded, tears filling his eyes. Tory's heart ached for him. All his young life he'd only known abandonment and rejection. How could he believe that anyone would love him? Suddenly she had a bright idea.

"Nelson, when is your birthday?" she asked.

Nelson turned his face away again. "I don't know," he murmured, so softly that Tory could barely hear him. "I don't even know how old I am."

Tory stood up straight. She didn't say anything else to Nelson about his birthday, but a plan began to form in her mind. She couldn't wait to tell Adam about it.

"Hey, where's my roofing partner?" Greg called from the ridge of the roof. Tory scurried back up the ladder to join him.

Instead of beginning Nelson's lesson, Adam rode Tamarindo over to the edge of the building closest to where Tory and Greg were working. "Hey, you guys, I have some bad news," he called up to them. "Mr. Allen says we're almost completely out of water. When he went into town to get some, none of the stores had any. He came back empty-handed."

Tory's mouth went dry at the thought of no drinking water. She knew the cistern water wasn't safe to drink and boiling water to drink was a long and tedious process for this many people.

Greg stood up and called out to all the students who were working in different parts of the orphanage grounds. "We have a problem, everyone," he shouted. "It's time to have a prayer meeting.

Everyone gathered around in a big circle and held hands, including Jenny, Dilma, Oscar, Carlitos, and Nelson. "Father," Greg prayed, "we need water to be able to continue this work for You. We know You are able to supply all our needs, so we're lifting our hearts to You together right now, asking You to provide us with drinking water. Thank You for Your loving care for us. We love You. In Jesus' name we ask this favor. Amen."

They returned to work, but Tory noticed that Greg took fewer drinks from the water supply. Adam held back, too, and she knew that both of the guys were leaving as much of the remaining water as possible for the others.

By late morning the searing heat made it impossible to work on the roof. Tory climbed down and joined the rest of the group in the shade. She dampened her shirt tail with water and wiped it over her parched lips.

As the rumble of a big truck filled the air, everyone stood up and peered down the lane to see who was coming. As the truck topped the hill, Tory saw five-gallon jugs of crystal-clear water bouncing around on a tall rack on the back. The truck pulled up in front of the orphanage and the driver got out. Tory recognized him as the owner of the largest water bottler in the area. She'd seen him on previous trips to obtain drinking water for the orphanage.

"I thought you might need some water," he said simply. "There's no water available in town, so I was sure you'd be running out. Take all you need. It's my gift to you."

Adam and Greg stared at each other in surprise, then ran to unload the water from the truck. The others joined them until enough clear, cold water sat in jugs in the courtyard to last for several weeks.

"Gracias, gracias," the group called after the man as he drove away. Then they joined hands in another circle, this time to thank God for His gift of life-giving water. Tory saw tears in many of the students' eyes as they re-

alized what a miracle had been worked just for them.

Two days before the group was scheduled to leave, Tory convinced Adam to slip away to town with her to buy party supplies. Like two kids in a candy store, they ran from shop to shop, picking out party hats, noise-makers, Mexican pastries, and special containers of juice, enough for the whole group. Adam came out of a bakery carrying a huge cake with the words "Happy Birthday, Nelson" written on top in bright-blue icing.

They hauled the supplies back to the main house and set it all up on the front porch. When they'd strung streamers and party lights and fastened bright-colored balloons to the pillars, Tory stood back to admire their handiwork.

"Perfect," she pronounced. "Nelson will love it."

Adam walked up to the orphanage to alert the group to sneak down to the house, then he caught Tamarindo and saddled him as if he were meeting Nelson for his regularly scheduled riding lesson. Then he cantered the gelding up the road to the orphanage.

A few minutes later Tory saw him heading for the river at a full gallop with Nelson crouched behind the saddle, clinging to Adam's back. She smiled to herself as she thought of how surprised Nelson would be when he found out where Adam was *really* taking him.

As soon as Adam and Nelson were out of sight, the group streamed down the hill and gathered quickly on the lawn.. Dilma jumped up and down, squealing with excitement. Just then Tamarindo thundered into the yard and skidded to a stop right in front of the table that held the huge birthday cake.

"Happy birthday to you, Happy birthday to you, Happy Birthday, dear Nelson, Happy birthday to you," the group sang in Spanish. Nelson slipped to the ground and walked slowly over to the cake, his eyes wide. Then he sat down on the ground and burst into tears.

Tory hurried to his side and hugged him close. He gazed up at her and said, "I'm not crying because I'm sad, Tory. I'm crying because this is the happiest day of my life."

On the last night of the meetings, Greg made an appeal to the congregation for each person to make a decision about what he or she was going to do with their life. Would it be surrendered to Jesus and lived in response to His love or would it be lived in selfishness? He invited all those who wished to give their lives to Jesus through the power of the Holy Spirit, to come forward.

Without hesitation, Maria stepped up to the front of the church, tears streaming down her cheeks. She knelt just in front of the rough wooden podium. Tory slipped to her side and placed an arm around her shoulders. Then, out of the corner of her eye, she saw a man take his place beside them. He bent down to pray, and Tory heard deep sobs wrack his body.

It wasn't until the prayer time was over, and she stood with Maria to walk back to her seat, that Tory looked fully into the man's face. With a wave of shock she realized that it was the man with the machete that had stood in the path that day she rode to the river with Nelson. But instead of the evil leer she'd seen on his face before, he had a new light in his eyes and a sense of peace in his expression.

Wow, what a change, she thought. *Thank You, Father, for such a miracle as this! This is even more amazing than providing water for us.* How much greater miracle could there be than a completely changed life?

Tory rode with the rest of the group to the orphanage but decided to walk the rest of the way to the fish hatchery. It had been such an eventful evening, she wanted time to process her feelings about it.

"Do you mind if I walk with you?"

She looked up to see Greg, his tie in his hand, walking across the lawn toward her.

"Not at all." She smiled at him. "I'd love the chance to talk with you."

They walked in silence for awhile, each deep in their own thoughts. Then Greg spoke. "We have only one more day here, Tory," he said solemnly. "I want to tell you something. Please don't say anything until I'm all finished."

Tory gulped and nodded, wondering what Greg wanted to say to her that was so important. "Go ahead. I'm listening."

"We've been working side by side for weeks and I've been watching you," Greg said carefully. He paused, as if thinking, then continued in a very serious voice. "My life as a pastor will not be an easy one. It will be filled with heavy responsibility and hardship. I know that I need a life partner that understands the solemn times we live in and the importance of telling the world about Jesus and His soon return. I want to ask you if you would consider a serious relationship with me, to see if we are compatible enough to think of a future together."

He reached out and took her hand, squeezing it gently. "What do you think? Is there any possibility?"

Tory walked along without speaking for a long time. She didn't pull her hand back, but her thoughts tumbled over each other in a mass of confusion. She really liked Greg. She liked his eyes, his smile, his gentle spirit, his strong commitment to God.

"I won't say 'no,'" she said finally. "I just can't for sure say 'yes.'"

Adam was standing under a *ciruela* tree in front of the fish hatchery dormitory as Tory and Greg walked up the hill hand in hand. The deepening shadows concealed his face so she couldn't see his expression, but he turned quickly and disappeared into his room. Tory didn't see him again for the rest of the evening.

CHAPTER FOURTEEN

In the weeks following the university students' return to the U.S., the drought worsened. Day after sizzling hot day the sun pounded down from a cloudless bronze sky. Siesta time stopped being a luxury to Tory and became an absolute necessity because it was simply too hot to move in the suffocating heat of early afternoon.

Greg called frequently from the United States. Tory looked forward to his calls and enjoyed talking to him, but something held her back from making any promises. Every evening, just before sunset, she and Adam walked up to the new water tank and climbed on top, letting their legs dangle over the sides. They watched the sky shift into its nighttime colors, from blue to lavender and gold and then to deep purple.

"There's the first star," Adam called out, as they lay on their backs staring up at the sky one evening in early March. "I get to make a wish."

Tory sat up and threw a little pebble at Adam. It hit him right on the top of his head. "So, what did you wish for?" she asked, teasing him.

"I can't tell you. It won't come true if I do," Adam said. He grabbed her foot and pulled off her shoe, tickling the bottom of her foot unmercifully.

"Uh, let me guess. Does it have something to do with a certain girl named Jodie?"

Adam shook his head. "No. We wrote for awhile

and then just stopped. Something wasn't quite right. I'm not sure what."

Tory could feel Adam's gaze even in the deepening twilight. She felt suddenly self-conscious. "Oh," she said simply.

"What about you and Greg?"

Tory shrugged. "He calls at least once a week. I like him."

"You like him. Hm-m-m." Adam cleared his throat as if he wanted to say more. Then he stood up. "Hey, it's getting dark. We'd better get back."

The next morning, Mr. Allen gathered the whole group for worship. Antonio, Flor, Linda Allen, Tory, Adam, and the children sat in a circle for Bible reading and prayer.

Mr. Allen's face looked grim as he opened his Bible to 1 Kings 18 and read the story of the drought in Israel. "Just as Elijah prayed for rain back then, we must pray for rain now. Water is running low and the fields are tinder dry. One spark and the countryside could go up in smoke."

Dilma and Jenny climbed up into Tory's lap. Even though Mr. Allen spoke in English and they couldn't understand many of his words, the look of concern on his face told them something was seriously wrong. Tory hugged them close, burying her face in Jenny's soft, fuzzy hair.

When she walked out to the pasture to take Tamarindo his daily chunks of apple, Tory noticed the withered, dry grass in the pasture with alarm. The gelding galloped over to the fence to greet her. He snorted and nuzzled her hand eagerly.

"Hey, big boy." She held her hand out flat with the apples on her palm and let the horse gobble them up. "You are such a glutton."

She slipped through the fence and ran her hand along Tamarindo's beautiful neck, and down his withers, across his back and along his hindquarters. Even with the drought, the horse hadn't dropped any weight. Every muscle rippled with strength and his coat glowed with a healthy sheen. She knew Adam had been taking the horse out to search for better grazing every day since the grass in the pasture dried up. She had a sneaking suspicion he was supplementing his diet with dried corn, also.

She pressed her face into Tamarindo's mane, her arms around his neck. "You don't know how lucky you are to have someone that cares about you so much," she whispered. "Lots of other horses are very hungry right now."

Adam, she thought, smiling to herself. *Dear, sweet, funny, adventurous Adam.* She tried to picture what her life was like before Adam came into it, but it seemed he had always been there. She couldn't imagine going through a single day without him in it.

A stiff wind sprang up from the west blowing twigs and bunches of dried grass across the pasture. Tamarindo tossed his head, pulling away from Tory and pacing up and down the fence. He snorted nervously and stopped every few steps to paw the ground.

"What's wrong with you, boy?" Tory sprinted out to the center of the pasture where she could see the surrounding mountains better, and scanned the horizon. The wind picked up, howling ominously through the trees and kicking up miniature dust devils in the bone dry earth.

She turned back to the east and gasped in horror. The mountains on the far side of the valley were hidden behind a wall of smoke and flames. She hadn't smelled the smoke because of the direction of the wind. Right now it was blowing the fire away from the orphanage.

Tory wheeled around and ran for the gate to warn the others. Then she stopped dead in her tracks. *Tamarindo*. If she left him in the pasture and the wind changed, he could be trapped by the fire.

Dear God, please don't let the wind change direction, she prayed as she ran to the shed and grabbed Tamarindo's bridle. The horse seemed to sense the urgency of the situation and allowed Tory to slip the bridle over his head without any trouble. She flipped the reins over his neck and jumped up on his back.

"Come on, Tamarindo," she urged, leaning low on his neck and urging him into a full gallop toward the gate. "We have to get down to the orphanage *pronto*."

Adam and Mr. Allen met her on the road before she even reached the orphanage. The expressions on their grimy, sweat-streaked faces were tight with concern. Tory slipped from Tamarindo's back and led him the rest of the way, quickening her stride to keep up with the two men.

"I'm glad you brought Tamarindo," Adam said, glancing back at the eastern sky. "I just don't have a very good feeling about this fire. The countryside is far too dry and that wind could shift at a moment's notice."

Mr. Allen nodded grimly. "We'll soak everything we can to try to protect it, but our water supply is pretty low. I don't know how much good it will do."

When they reached the courtyard, Tory tied Tamarindo to a pillar and looked around for the children. She found them huddled in a circle with Flor in one of the dormitory rooms. Their eyes were shut tight and hands folded in prayer. A lump rose in Tory's throat as she heard Dilma's lisping prayer in Spanish, pleading with God to keep the fire away from the orphanage.

Tory and Adam scrounged up every bucket they could find and started to work, along with Mr. Allen, Antonio, and Linda, filling them with water and placing them around the outside of the buildings. Tory glanced at the corncrib and the rice storage area as she hurried by. With a sinking heart she realized that the whole food supply for the orphanage was in grave danger.

Suddenly Tory heard a shout from the garden area. She ran out of the courtyard and around the building to see Nelson pointing at the hillside to the west. There, directly upwind from the orphanage, a column of smoke and flames leaped into the air.

Tory screamed for the others. Within seconds, Adam and Mr. Allen stood beside her, staring in horror at the advancing fire.

"God help us," Mr. Allen gasped. "We're surrounded. Whichever way the wind shifts, the fire will still reach us." He dropped to his knees. Tory, Adam, and Nelson knelt with him.

"Father," Mr. Allen prayed. "This is a hopeless situation for us right now. We are pleading with You to step in and save us. This orphanage is Yours and all of us are in Your hands."

Adam's voice joined Mr. Allen's. "We're asking for a miracle, Lord," he pleaded. "We need rain right now."

"Amen," Tory whispered, her heart pounding as the acrid smell of smoke filled her nose. She opened her eyes and saw that Flor and the rest of the children had joined them. Carlitos watched the advancing fire with wide, solemn eyes. Jenny whimpered softly and toddled to Adam's side, lifting her arms to be picked up.

Just as the fire reached the ridge directly behind the water tower, Tory felt something splash on her neck. She reached back and felt the spot, then looked up at the sky. A dark cloud hovered overhead and more drops fell.

"It's raining!" she shouted, jumping up and down in a circle, laughing and crying all at the same time. All the children yelled and held up their hands as the rain began to fall harder and harder. No one ran for shelter, they just stood in the rain and let the cool water drench their clothes and soak their hair.

"Everyone join hands," Mr. Allen called out, water running down his face and dripping off his chin. He led the group in a prayer of thanksgiving and praise.

The flames on the mountainside went out quickly in the rainstorm. When the downpour ended, Tory and Adam untied Tamarindo and led him back down to his pasture. The rain mixed with the dusty dry earth had transformed the pasture into a giant mud hole, but Tamarindo didn't seem to mind at all. As soon as Adam released him, he ran across the field, kicking up his heels, then he dropped to the ground and rolled in the thick mud.

"His own mother wouldn't recognize him now," Tory chortled. "What a muddy mess." She glanced at Adam, then started backing away from him as she saw the mischievous look on his face. "Oh, no you don't, Adam Hartman."

She started to run, but Adam caught her and deftly flipped her down into one of the muckiest mud holes in the field. She grabbed handfuls of mud and threw them at him, plastering his T-shirt with it. Soon they were both covered with mud from head to toe.

"Tory, telephone," she heard Linda call from the front porch of the main house.

Tory looked at Adam and giggled. "Oops," she said. "I don't think Linda will want me in the house like this."

"Nope," Adam chuckled. "Here, let me help you." He grabbed Tamarindo's water bucket and held it over

Tory's head, dumping the cold water over her. Tamarindo snorted and tossed his head. "Sorry, boy," Adam said. "I'll replace it, I promise."

Tory tried to wring as much water out of her clothes as she could as she ran to the house. Linda met her at the door with a towel and she wrapped it around herself, kicking off her shoes on the porch. She hurried to the phone.

"Hello, this is Greg," a familiar voice spoke on the other end of the line. "What were you doing?"

Tory gulped. "Uh, having a mud fight with Adam. We just had this big fire and we prayed and it started to rain and, uh—"

"I see," Greg said. A long silence followed. When he spoke again, his voice sounded strained. "Tory, you're going to have to choose between me and Adam, you know."

"W-what do you mean?" Tory felt her throat tighten. "Adam is my best friend. I can't choose you over him. It just wouldn't be fair."

There was another long pause. "What's not fair is that you are not putting your whole heart into our relationship," Greg said sadly. "Think about it, Tory. It's your choice. You're going to have to make it."

Tory heard a click, then the dial tone. It took a few seconds for her to realize that Greg had just hung up on her. She held the phone receiver in her hand and stared at it for awhile. Then she slowly returned it to the phone cradle.

Greg says I have to choose between him and Adam, Father, Tory prayed. *But that's silly because Adam is just a friend and has made it clear that he wants our relationship to stay that way.* She sighed heavily. She thought of everything she and Adam had been through over the last few months: finding Jenny and nursing her back to health, Douglas' death and funeral, riding

Tamarindo together all through the countryside, adventures to the river, singing, praying together. *I know one thing for sure, if I have to choose between a romantic relationship with Greg and my friendship with Adam, I choose Adam.*

The phone rang again and Tory picked it up, fully expecting it to be Greg again. "Hello," she said flatly. "This is Tory."

"Tory!" a joyful girl's voice cried on the other end of the line. "This is Robyn!"

"Robyn!" Tory shrieked. "I can't believe it's you. I have *so much* to tell you."

"Well, you'll have plenty of time to fill me in because I'm coming down for a week to see you. Is that OK?" She chuckled. "It better be, 'cause I already bought my plane ticket. I'll be there the first of April."

"Are you kidding? Of course it's OK." Tory laughed. "Adam and I will treat you to a week you'll never forget. We'll even take you riding."

"Hm-m-m. Adam, huh? I take it you two became friends instead of enemies."

Tory felt herself blushing. She was glad Robyn couldn't see her face. "Yes. We're friends," she said quietly.

"All right, I can tell by the tone that there is more to this story than meets the ear. I have to meet this guy."

Tory looked down at the floor and realized water was dripping from her clothes. Clumps of mud still clung to her hair. "Robyn, I need to go," she said, swiping the towel across her forehead. "My ears are full of mud, and I'm making a puddle.

"OK," Robyn said, a puzzled tone in her voice. "Are you all right?"

Tory smiled into the phone. "Yep," she said. "And I

can't wait to see you. Bring me some pictures of Peaches and Poppyseed, will you?"

"Sure will."

As soon as she hung up the phone, Tory ran outside to tell Adam about Robyn's visit.

"Isn't that the friend that you gave your horses to when you left to come here?" Adam asked, still digging mud from his clothes and hair. Tory nodded.

"Well," he said, "we'll have to make sure she has an unforgettable week. What do you think about a trip to the islands?"

"You mean snorkeling around Utila?" Tory's eyes widened in excitement. She'd heard of the crystal clear water around the Bay Islands that served as home to hundreds of species of bright-colored fish and other sea creatures. "Sounds perfect."

Adam picked up Tamarindo's empty bucket and headed for the cistern. "Guess I'd better keep my promise and refill this," he said. Then he turned to Tory and gave her a wry smile. "I thought that would be Greg calling you."

Tory gulped. "It was. The first call anyway." She stared at the ground. "He told me I had to choose between you and him. He told me I was being unfair to him to have such a close friendship with you."

"He's right, you know," Adam said softly. "But he could never love you as much as I do. He's never chased fireflies with you. He's never been on *any* adventures with you." He shook his head. "He doesn't know you like I do. You're my best friend in the world."

Tears welled up in Tory's eyes. She felt her heart pounding in her chest. She smiled weakly at Adam and reached up to brush a clump of mud from one of his eyebrows.

"You're my best friend, too," she said. "I love you, too."

CHAPTER FIFTEEN

From the moment they picked her up at the airport in San Pedro Sula, Robyn and Adam talked and joked together like old friends. On the long bus ride over to the coastal town of La Ceiba, Robyn filled Tory in on what had happened with Peaches and Poppyseed since she left Arkansas.

"You won't believe how much Poppyseed has developed," Robyn exclaimed. "He's past 2 now, you know, and he's as big as Peaches."

Tory shook her head. It was hard to believe that the frisky little foal she'd delivered what seemed like such a short time ago, was already almost grown. "These children just grow up too fast these days."

"So tell me about this marvelous Tamarindo you've been writing to me about," Robyn said. "I can't wait to see him."

Adam leaned forward, his eyes sparkling with pride. "He's the best horse in the world," he said. "Smartest, fastest, prettiest . . ."

"Whoa, there." Robyn laughed. "Are you sure this is an objective opinion? How do you know he's all those things?"

"Because I know what I like." Adam glanced at Tory with a strange, determined expression on his face. Robyn caught the look and raised her eyebrows at Tory. Tory just blushed and looked out the window. "We-e-l-l,"

Robyn said with a dramatic flourish, "obviously there's a *lot* you have to catch me up on, Tory."

The bus pulled up into the station in La Ceiba. Tory stared out the window at the huge crowd milling around the station. Moms with babies in their arms, tattooed young men with cigarettes hanging from their mouths, the ever-present throng of street children. Tory had never seen such a kaleidoscope of faces.

Adam led the way as they pushed through the jostling crowd to a row of taxis parked along a side street waiting for passengers. One of the drivers, a young man who looked to be the same age as Adam, jumped from his taxi as soon as he saw them and opened the passenger door wide. With a sweeping bow, he said in Spanish, "Come with me, Senor and Senoritas. My taxi is the best."

Tory liked the young man at once. She nodded to Robyn and Adam and they all piled into the little blue station wagon. Robyn looked around at all the other taxis parked along the street, every one of them an old Datsun or Toyota. "Now I know what happens to all the old foreign cars in the U.S.," she said, giggling. "They come here and start all over."

Adam struck up a conversation with the taxi driver, who introduced himself as "Rudy." Adam told Rudy they were headed for the island of Utila. Rudy shook his head dubiously. "The boat that usually takes tourists to the islands was badly damaged in a big storm last week," he said. "It will not be repaired for at least two more weeks. If you want to go to the islands, you will have to go to the docks and see if one of the traders will let you ride on his cargo boat." Rudy drove them straight to the docks and waited while Adam sprinted up the whole length of the dock. He talked with every boat captain and soon came back, a dejected look on his face.

"No one is going until tomorrow. We'll have to find a place to stay tonight."

Rudy laughed. "Not a very good chance of finding a room here," he said. "But I know of a hotel that is a little out of the way, and we'll see if there is a room for you there. It's on the beach."

"Uh, we need two rooms," Adam added. Rudy laughed again and shook his head.

Adam turned to Tory and Robyn. "Pray with me, OK? I know God can provide us with a place to stay."

Tory and Robyn nodded and together they offered a prayer, asking for a room for the night and protection for their trip. Soon the taxi pulled up in front of a bright pink building with clean white trim. Statues of flamingos stood in the sandy courtyard and colorful hammocks hung between stately palms. Tory could see the beach just beyond the building.

"I *like* this place," she whispered to Robyn. "I hope they have room for us."

The owner of the hotel came out of the office when he saw Adam approaching. Tory could see the man shaking his head. Then the phone rang and the man disappeared in the office for a few moments. When he returned, he had a look of surprise on his face. He held two sets of keys out to Adam and pointed to the two doors closest to the courtyard.

Adam handed the man some money, then ran back to the taxi. "Wow!" he said, his eyes shining. "That was one of the fastest answers to prayer I've ever seen. We have our two rooms and for *half price*. Someone from the city who had already paid for two rooms had an emergency come up and won't be able to come until tomorrow. Because the rooms were already paid for once, the owner gave them to us for half!"

Rudy grinned. "I brought you to a good place, no?" He helped Tory and Robyn unload their bags, then hopped back into his taxi. "Tomorrow very early I will be back to take you to the docks," he said and drove away.

After getting settled in their rooms, Tory and Robyn headed for the beach to watch the sunset. Adam joined them, and the threesome strolled arm in arm along the long stretch of sand.

"I wish the kids could be here," Tory said wistfully, picturing Dilma and Jenny splashing happily in the waves and Oscar and Nelson building forts out of driftwood. "They'd love it."

Robyn gave Tory a quizzical look. "What are you going to do when you have to go back to the U.S. and leave them?" she asked. "Have you thought about it?"

Tory felt as if something was reaching right into her heart and ripping it, as she thought about what Robyn was saying. She knew she wouldn't be staying at the orphanage forever; her assignment had been for just a year. But how could she leave the children?

"They'll have Flor and Antonio," she said, fighting back the tears. "And I know someone else will come to take my place."

She felt Adam's arm around her waist squeeze her tightly. "Yeah, it's going to be really hard to leave," he said. Tory could hear the same wrenching pain in his voice. "Especially Nelson." He shook his head as if he could shake away the hurt. "But my year is up soon too."

"What are you going to do, Adam?" Robyn asked. She pulled Tory and Adam around and plopped down in the sand, forcing them down with her. They sat facing the ocean and watched pelicans diving for fish in the calm gray water.

Adam paused for a few minutes, deep in thought. When he spoke, Tory could hear an edge of excitement in his voice. "I had a phone call last week from some friends, and . . . well, I'm going to northern Idaho for awhile." He seemed uncomfortable, but hurried on. "I've been offered a place up there, caretaking a lodge right on the Canadian border. It's a retreat setting and people come there to rest and get away from it all. I have enough psychology classes that it won't take me much more to get a degree in counseling, so I want to do this for a couple years to get the experience."

Tory stared at Adam in surprise. "You never told me this! That's incredible. What an adventure."

"So you don't think I'm crazy?" Adam picked up a handful of sand and let it run slowly through his fingers.

"Are you kidding? I'd give my right arm to live in a place like that."

"Really?" Adam grinned. "That wouldn't be such a good idea. It's pretty rugged living and right arms are very important in such surroundings."

Tory picked up a handful of sand and poured it down the back of Adam's shirt. "You know what I mean."

Robyn stood up, laughing heartily. "You two are a pair, I'll say."

The next morning, true to his word, Rudy pulled up in front of the hotel in his taxi. He helped the girls load their backpacks into the back of the station wagon, whistling a Spanish love song as he worked. He and Adam kept up a lively conversation all the way to the docks.

"*Adios,* my friends," he said as he dropped them off in front of one of the cargo boats. "I will be here day after tomorrow when the boat comes back. I'll pick you up and take you to the bus."

The cargo boat wasn't much bigger than a small tug boat, but Tory noticed that every square inch of deck space was filled with something. Piles of lumber, no doubt destined to become part of some islander's new house, covered the floor. Huge mesh bags of cabbages and carrots filled every remaining nook and cranny. A small pink pig sat in a corner, tied to one of the boat railings.

Tory and Robyn found a stack of boxes to sit on and propped their feet up on one of the bags of carrots as the boat churned its way out of the harbor and into the open sea. A mattress set balanced precariously on top of a stack of lumber beside them, its protective plastic cover torn to shreds. Three young boys whom Tory had seen working with the captain getting the boat ready to sail, lounged on the mattress, talking incessantly in some strange island lingo that sounded like a mix of Spanish, British, and Indian words.

Robyn leaned over and whispered to Tory, "I feel sorry for whoever is getting that mattress set. It isn't exactly getting treated with kid gloves."

Just then Adam poked his head around the corner from his spot in the front of the boat. "Come up here, you two. I want to show you something."

Tory and Robyn clambered over the cargo to reach the spot where Adam stood holding onto the railing as the boat swayed and rocked in the ocean swells. Adam pointed into the swells between the waves. "Watch right there and tell me what you see."

Suddenly a huge flock of what looked to Tory like tiny silver birds flitted along the surface of the swell in a graceful water ballet. Within seconds, they disappeared into the ocean.

Puzzled, Tory turned to Adam. "I didn't know birds could swim like that. Did you see that flock of birds dive right into the water?"

Adam doubled over laughing and Robyn joined him. Tory frowned at them both. "What is so funny?"

"They're *fish,* Tory," Robyn said, still laughing. *"Flying* fish." She pointed to the waves beside the boat where the little silver creatures flashed in the sunlight. "See, there they are again."

Tory shook her head. "Well I'll be a monkey's uncle," she muttered. "I've heard of flying fish, but I had no idea they looked like *that."*

It took the heavily loaded cargo boat three hours to reach the island. By the time the boat bumped its way up to the Utila dock, Tory and Robyn were shivering in their clothes, soaked by the salty spray of the waves.

"I hope we can find a room here," Adam said as he looked around the crowded dock. "There are a lot of people here for the holiday."

A man from the boat walked up just then and extended his hand in greeting. "I am Emilio," he said with a friendly smile. "I saw you on the boat. I must tell you that this island is very full this week. There is no room in any of the hotels. But I will take you to a place that may have room for you."

Tory and Robyn looked at each other and then at Adam. Adam pressed his hands together in a praying gesture just for a second to signal the girls to be in prayer. "OK", he said. "We will follow you."

Emilio led them up the main street of the little island town, then turned on a sidewalk that soon became nothing more than a jungle path. They hiked deeper and deeper into the jungle. Tiny flies landed on Tory's legs, biting her viciously. She noticed Robyn and Adam slapping at their arms and legs and knew that they were under attack too.

Just when Tory was sure they were being led into the middle of nowhere, a clearing appeared. Neatly painted cottages held high above the ground by sturdy wooden stilts stood in a semicircle around a central garden area. Bright pink and red tropical flowers bloomed along trim walkways.

Tory heard Robyn gasp in surprise. "Who would have ever guessed this place was here," she exclaimed.

Adam followed Emilio into the main office. When he returned, he was grinning from ear to ear. "You'll never believe this one," he said. "They are full for the holiday week, too. Everyone books these rooms months ahead. *But* it just so happens that they have two rooms that they aren't quite finished with. They have to install the propane stoves in the kitchenettes. They were supposed to have the rooms ready last week but were delayed by the storms. They said if we want to stay in the rooms they'll let us have them for *half price* since they have to come in and work on them a little while we're here."

"Woo hoo!" Tory shouted. "Our heavenly Father comes through again!" She grabbed Robyn's hands and the two of them did a little victory dance right there in front of the hotel. Emilio stood back and watched their happiness with a satisfied smile on his face.

Minutes later, as they were hauling their gear into their rooms, Tory suddenly remembered that they hadn't thanked Emilio for leading them to the hotel. She ran outside and checked the garden area and the office, but he was nowhere to be seen. She asked the woman at the desk in the office if she knew where the man who had led them here had gone. The woman just shook her head. "I didn't see any man," she said. "Just you and your friends."

Puzzled, Tory ran out to the main path but it

stretched on through the jungle, empty. She stood in the middle of the trail and scratched her head. Where could he have disappeared to so quickly? Then the possibility began to dawn on her that their benefactor may not have been a man at all. *Father, did You send Emilio to help us find our way to a safe place to stay on this island?* she prayed. *Is he really an angel?*

She listened intently for an answer, but all she heard was the rustling of the thick tropical foliage around her and the soft twittering of the birds in the trees.

CHAPTER SIXTEEN

All the next day, the trio snorkeled in the crystal-clear water of the Blue Bayou. Fish of every size, flashing stripes and spots of brilliant blue, red, purple, and yellow, darted in and out of the coral reef below them.

"Hey," Tory called to Adam as she raised her head to check the others' whereabouts, "I feel as if I'm swimming in some giant's aquarium. I keep expecting a huge hand to scoop me up out of the water, thundering, 'What do you think you're doing in my fish tank?'"

Adam laughed and nodded in agreement. "Yep. It's pretty amazing down there. I just saw a moray eel."

Robyn swam close to where Tory was treading water and held her hand out. An exquisite cowry shell rested in her palm, its shimmering chocolate brown surface accented with creamy white spots.

"Isn't it the most beautiful thing you've ever seen?" Robyn whispered, an awestruck tone in her voice. "I'm going to take it home with me so I never forget how incredibly gorgeous this place is."

Later that evening, after they'd taken showers and rubbed aloe vera ointment into their sunburns, Tory, Robyn, and Adam hiked back into town. A sweet aroma filled the air and they followed it to a little bakery tucked on a side street near the docks. "Coconut bread!" Tory exclaimed, as she spied the fresh loaves cooling on racks on the counter. "Let's get some."

Robyn pointed to a sign that advertised what cold drinks were available. "What is tamarindo?"

"You simply *must* try it, my dear," Adam said with mock formality. "Allow me to buy you a glass. No visit to Central America is complete without a taste of the highly acclaimed tamarindo."

Robyn gave Tory a puzzled look. "Isn't that the name of your horse at the orphanage? He's named after a *fruit drink?*"

Adam and Tory burst out laughing. "Yes," Tory said. "And I must say, now that I know him, that it fits him well. Wait 'til you taste it and then meet Tamarindo and you'll see. Tart and sassy but sweet. Unique. Unforgettable."

"Kind of like you," Adam said, grinning impishly at Tory.

The trip back to Santa Barbara the next day went smoothly. A ferryboat took the trio back to La Ceiba where Rudy, true to his word, waited in his little blue taxi to transport them to the bus station. He waved goodbye as they boarded the bus, shouting, "I'll see you next time you come to the coast, *amigos.*"

It was after dark when they pulled up to the orphanage, but the children were all waiting for them with hugs and kisses and lots of stories to tell of all that had happened while Tory and Adam were gone. They all loved Robyn at once. Jenny climbed up in her lap and wouldn't budge even when tempted with a fresh mango.

The next morning Tory and Adam took Robyn down to the pasture to meet Tamarindo. Before she even had a chance to call the gelding, he spotted them and galloped up to the fence.

"Wow." Robyn stood transfixed, staring at the

horse. "You're right. He's magnificent."

Tamarindo tossed his head, his thick, dark mane glistening in the early morning sunlight. The muscles in his thick chest rippled as he pawed the ground, impatient for his apple chunks.

Tory laughed. "OK, OK." She started to offer the apples to the horse, then stopped. "Here, Robyn, you give them to him."

Robyn took the apple pieces and held out her hand. Tamarindo sniffed her briefly, then gobbled up the apples as if he'd known Robyn all his life. She giggled. "I guess the way to a *horse's* heart is through his stomach, too."

Adam saddled Tamarindo and let Robyn ride him all over the pasture, then out along the path and down to the river. When she returned, her face shone with exhilaration. "This is heaven," she sighed, gazing around at the beautiful countryside and gently stroking Tamarindo's sleek neck. "I don't see how it can get any better than this. So this is the 'difficult' life in the mission field? Looks pretty good to me. I can't imagine anything bad happening here."

Tory and Adam exchanged knowing glances. She knew Robyn would never understand the pain and fear they'd faced over the last year even if she tried to explain it to her. But Adam did. She realized as she looked into his eyes that she had changed since coming to Honduras. That she would never be the same again. And only Adam understood.

The week ended far too soon. Mr. Allen loaned Adam the Ford to take Robyn back to the airport so they wouldn't have to catch a bus. As they stood waiting for the plane, Tory hugged Robyn tightly, fighting back the tears. "I'll see you soon," she said sadly. "Kiss Peaches and Poppyseed for me."

Robyn gave Adam a hug, too. "Take good care of my best friend," she told him sternly and turned to board the plane.

"I will," Adam called after her.

Tory and Adam rode in silence as they left the city and headed cross-country back to the orphanage. Suddenly Adam whipped the truck around and took a road to the north that wound along the shoreline of a huge, shining lake. He pulled into the parking lot of a restaurant on stilts with a deck that jutted out right over the water.

"Let's eat here," he said.

Tory loved the little restaurant, with its red and white checked oilcloth tablecloths and ever-present jars of hot onion relish. They chose a table near the deck so they could watch the pelicans and other birds wheeling and diving over the water. Tory ordered bean soup with cabbage salad, and Adam had *baliadas*—Honduran burritos with a special white cream filling that tasted like cheese.

When they finished eating, Adam excused himself for a few minutes. Tory could see him talking earnestly with the owner of the restaurant. He returned with a huge smile on his face.

"How would you like to take a boat ride on the lake?" he asked, excitement in his voice. "I have a rowboat arranged for. We can go right now."

The lake was glassy smooth as they rowed out into the water. Peering over the edge of the boat Tory saw huge fish swimming languidly through waving underwater plants. She sighed contentedly.

"You know, it's funny," she said. "After everything we've been through here in Honduras, I think Robyn is right. It's not that difficult. Because God has a way of turning even the worst things that happen to us into blessings. Even Douglas' death. As horrible and painful as that was, it was the beginning of a new life for Maria." She trailed one hand in the cool lake water, leaving a miniature wake behind. "I think I'm beginning to understand a little about trusting God. After awhile, you begin to see that He *can* be trusted. There's no reason to be afraid."

Adam sat quietly for awhile, listening, holding the oars still and letting the boat drift. A gentle breeze sprang up just as the sun began to sink low in the west, sending golden shimmers along the ripples the wind created on the water.

When he finally spoke, his voice sounded somehow different than she had ever heard it before. "Tory," he said. "I need to talk to you about something important."

Tory nodded, wondering what could be so serious that Adam would bring her out into the middle of the lake to talk about it.

"I'm going to northern Idaho in June. It's going to be rough, living without electricity and heating with wood. There are wild animals like bear and cougar all around on the property."

"It sounds perfect," Tory said, giving Adam what she hoped was an encouraging smile. Inside, her heart sank as she thought of how far away he would be from her. Maybe so far away that she'd never see him again. Her mouth felt dry and a huge lump formed in her throat.

I can't let him know how much this hurts me, she thought. *This is important to him. This is not about me and how I feel about it.*

"Winters are harsh up there," he continued. "Last year they had 10 feet of snow with some drifts up to 30 feet deep. The water comes from a spring high on the hill and sometimes in the winter, when the animals are looking for running water to drink, they'll chew through the pipe and cut off the water supply to the cabin."

Adam paused and gave Tory a long look. "It's three miles just to the mailbox, then another 28 miles to the nearest *small* town. Pretty isolated, huh?"

"It sounds like it." Tory shifted on the hard boat seat, waiting for Adam to tell her his point in all this.

Reaching for her hand, Adam cleared his throat. "Tory, I was wrong about wanting our relationship to stay 'just friends.' I was afraid if we tried to make it more than that we'd lose what we have and I've never had a friend like you. We've been together through all kinds of amazing things this year and I don't want it to stop. *Ever.*"

He hurried on, as if trying to get the words out before he lost his courage. "I'm asking you to go with me to Idaho. I can't bear the thought of going anywhere without you. I know it's a lot to ask, going to such a remote area where who knows what we'll face. But it will be an adventure. And I can't think of a better adventure partner than you."

Tory stared at Adam, suddenly speechless. "Uh-h. Well, uh," she stammered. "I don't know what to say."

Scenes from the past year raced through her mind. The friendship they shared was deeper, unlike anything she'd ever experienced. She hadn't let herself feel it, much less think it. But it was love.

Sitting here in the boat, looking into Adam's eyes, she knew that she felt the same. That she'd felt this way for a long time; she'd just been afraid to face her feelings because she thought that Adam wanted only friendship.

"Then just say 'yes,'" Adam said softly. "Say you'll marry me and come with me to Idaho."

Father, is this where You've been leading us all along? Tory prayed. *Is Adam the one You've chosen for me to spend my life with?*

The golden sun sank below the trees and the sky burst into color. Rich pinks, reds, and purples streaked across the horizon. A flock of geese flew over, searching for a safe place to spend the night.

A thousand images flashed through Tory's mind: Adam riding Tamarindo, building the coffin for Douglas, holding Jenny tenderly in his arms, rescuing the doomed iguana, kneeling with her in prayer. Suddenly, she knew her answer. From the very deepest place in the bottom of her heart she gave it.

"Yes, Adam," she whispered. "I will."

HORSE HUSBANDRY HONORS

Here are the requirements for two horse honors as given in *Adventist Youth Honors,* copyright 1991 by the North American Division Church Ministries Department.

Horse Husbandry, Skill Level 1

1. What line of profit is derived by the use of specially-selected mares?

2. Why is it preferable to raise purebred colts rather than common grades?

3. Name at least five points that are desirable in selecting a horse.

4. What type of training will help colts to grow into gentle, dependable horses?

5. Describe the proper care and feeding of horses.

6. Know the parts of the following: halter, bridle, saddle.

7. Know how to properly put these items on a horse.

8. Know how to properly care for the hoofs of a horse. Know the parts of the hoof.

9. Care for one or more colts or horses over a period of six months.

Horsemanship (Instructor required)

1. Label on an outline drawing of a horse, or point out on a live horse a minimum of 30 different parts of a horse.

2. Label on an outline drawing or point out on a real saddle, a minimum of 10 parts of a Western saddle and nine parts of an English saddle. Label on an outline drawing, or point out on a real bridle, a minimum of six parts of a Western bridle and seven parts of an English bridle. Explain how to take care of your tack.

3. Describe the purpose of, and wear, a riding helmet and boots (or hard soled shoes with a heel) while working around horses and riding.

4. Describe and demonstrate three rules of safety in approaching and catching a horse.

5. Describe and demonstrate three rules of safety in leading a horse and show where the safest place is to stand around a horse.

6. Choose a safe place to tie a gentle horse, then demonstrate how to tie a gentle horse with a quick release manger knot, or bowline knot, demonstrating and explaining correct length of rope and height from the ground at which to tie.

7. Demonstrate and explain how to correctly groom a gentle horse.

8. Demonstrate and explain how to safely and correctly saddle and bridle a gentle horse.

9. Demonstrate and explain how to safely and correctly mount and dismount a gentle horse, and demonstrate a safe, well-balanced seat on a horse that is standing still.

10. Demonstrate and explain how to safely start, stop, and turn a gentle horse at walk, using leg, weight, voice, and rein aids.

11. Demonstrate and explain a correct leg-up mounting procedure on a bareback gentle horse that is standing quietly. Ride a gentle bareback horse for a minimum of 30 cumulative minutes at the walk, demonstrating good balance.

12. Demonstrate and explain good safety consciousness while riding a gentle horse with a minimum of one other rider. Demonstrate correct spacing, reversing direction, and passing other riders in an arena setting at the walk.

13. Negotiate a simple three element trail obstacle course set up on level ground, riding a gentle horse at the walk. Choose from:
    a. Step over log or pole, maximum height of 16 inches
    b. Pass between low barrels or bales of hay spaced 45 inches apart
    c. Zig-zag between poles set at 12-foot intervals
    d. Walk into a large key-hole (15-foot circle), turn and exit without stepping on or crossing any borderline.

14. Trail ride a gentle horse at the walk for a minimum of four cumulative hours.

15. Demonstrate and explain a minimum of three safety rules that apply to group trail rides.

POINTS OF THE HORSE

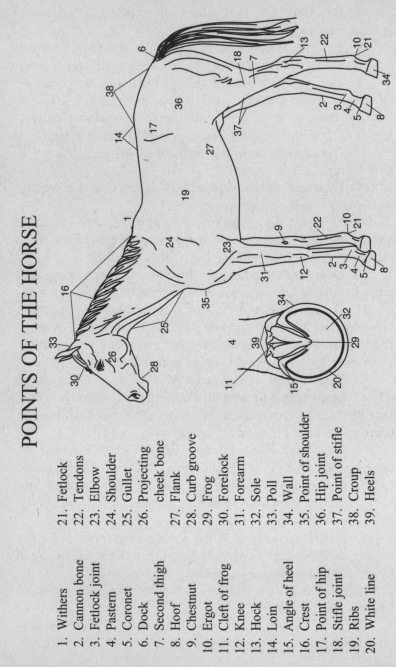

1. Withers
2. Cannon bone
3. Fetlock joint
4. Pastern
5. Coronet
6. Dock
7. Second thigh
8. Hoof
9. Chestnut
10. Ergot
11. Cleft of frog
12. Knee
13. Hock
14. Loin
15. Angle of heel
16. Crest
17. Point of hip
18. Stifle joint
19. Ribs
20. White line
21. Fetlock
22. Tendons
23. Elbow
24. Shoulder
25. Gullet
26. Projecting
    cheek bone
27. Flank
28. Curb groove
29. Frog
30. Forelock
31. Forearm
32. Sole
33. Poll
34. Wall
35. Point of shoulder
36. Hip joint
37. Point of stifle
38. Croup
39. Heels

WESTERN SADDLE

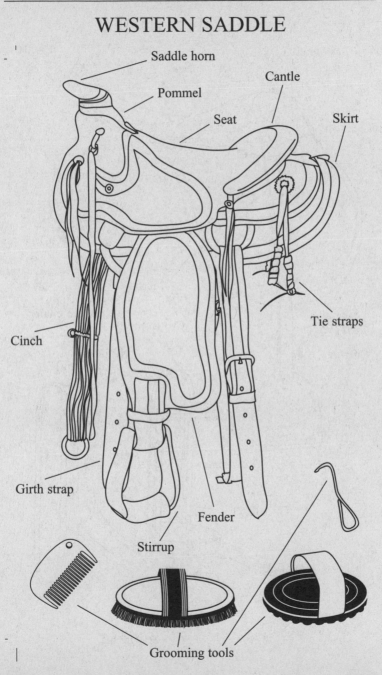

Saddle horn

Pommel

Cantle

Seat

Skirt

Tie straps

Cinch

Girth strap

Fender

Stirrup

Grooming tools

ENGLISH SADDLE

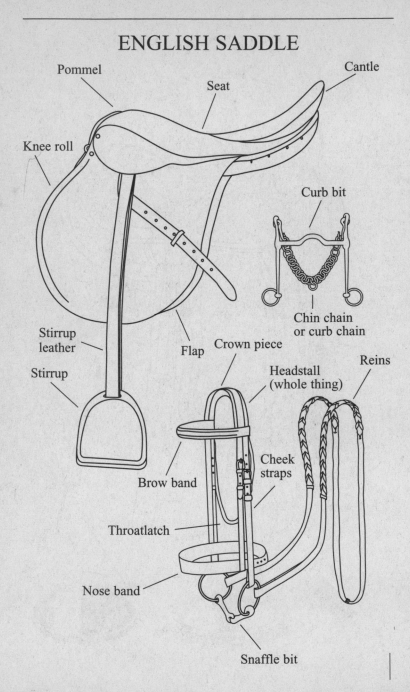

Pommel

Seat

Cantle

Knee roll

Curb bit

Chin chain
or curb chain

Stirrup
leather

Flap

Crown piece

Stirrup

Headstall
(whole thing)

Reins

Brow band

Cheek
straps

Throatlatch

Nose band

Snaffle bit